Moonlight F

Seven ...

By

M.L. Bullock

Dedication

To my husband, Kevin, the world's most devoted collector of ugly shirts. Thank you for all the plot twists, endless cups of coffee and those long back-road drives. Let the adventure continue. At last....

I saw the Pleiades through branches bare,
And close to mine your face
Soft glowing in the dark;
For Youth and Hope and Love and You were there
At our dear trysting-place
Arthur Henry Adams
Excerpt from "The Pleiades"

Chapter 1

The guesthouse looked like something out of a swanky coastal magazine. It was joined to the main house by a stepping-stone walkway lined with a few palm trees and interesting concrete statues of flamingos and dolphins. It was kitschy in a cool way, and I loved it instantly. I had never stayed at a beach house before.

Okay, Carrie Jo Jardine. You're here. Now what?

It was a surreal moment, not so much being at Ashland's place, I mean I'm no trembling wallflower when it came to guys, however the reason why I was here still shocked me. I was hiding from my former best friend who had just this knife came after me with a knife. And for whatever reason, she believed that the Beaumont fortune belonged to her which was so ridiculous of an idea I could barely quantify it.

Mia...what had happened to you?

Ashland said, "So, this guesthouse is only a few months old. As far as I know, you'll be the first one sleeping here, unless the housekeeper took an unauthorized nap." He sat on the bed and bounced on it a little to demonstrate its newness. I smiled at his thoughtfulness. Only a few people knew about my dream catching abilities; that I could see the past when I slept.

"Hey, get off there! I can't have you messing up my bed." I put my laptop and journals on the lovely white painted desk in front of the window and the rest of my things on the floor. I had a sudden thought. "Are any of these items antiques?"

"Nope. Nothing significant. Most of this is brand new. You should be safe here, Carrie Jo. I want you to get a good night's sleep."

"I plan on that. So why don't you take me on a tour, or do guests only get to see the guesthouse?"

He held my hands and kissed them. "I don't know what I would have done if something had happened to you tonight. I want you to promise me you'll be careful. No chances at all."

"Scout's honor," I said, but I had my fingers crossed behind my back. "Okay, let's walk and talk. You lead the way."

Ashland's home was remarkable. He had a leathery "man cave," with ridiculous overstuffed leather chairs and a massive television. I expected that, but he also had a gorgeous kitchen and a beautiful pool table. My eyes lit up when I saw it. I loved playing pool—it was the one sport I could win at. "Want to play?" I asked. He cast me a disbelieving look. "Oh, don't look so surprised. I'm good at quite a few sports," I lied. It was mostly pool and poker.

"Sure, rack 'em up." He grinned at me. "But I warn you, I'm pretty good."

"No, it's your table—you do the racking. Let's see how good you really are." He gave me a mock bow and racked up the balls.

"May I ask you something?" I reached into the netting to retrieve some of the balls and slung them his way.

"Yeah, sure. I'm an open book." He jostled the balls into the rack, tightening them and setting them on the mark. We perused a collection of sticks on an elegant wooden rack.

Choosing two of the most beautiful, we walked back to the table. He racked, so that meant I got to break. I lined up the cue ball on the opposite dot and had my eye on the 7 ball. I took aim at the 2 ball. I liked breaking left of center—it worked well for me. I had distributed the balls well with that first shot.

I shook my head. "There's something I can't figure out. Why did Mia believe she had a right to any jewelry that we might recover? I mean, she wasn't interested in stealing it—she really believes it belongs to her. Why? Do you know something about that, or is this another mystery? Like we need one more."

"I was surprised to hear that. I have to be honest, though; people file papers all the time claiming to be related to me somehow. I am extremely wealthy, and people are extremely greedy. If they can find a way to relieve you of your cash, they will do it. If she was making a claim that she was a relative, and went the legal way, there might be paperwork on it filed downtown. Hollis used to take care of those things for me."

"Hmm...it might be worth looking into. She's not the kind of girl to make something up like that." He looked at me with raised eyebrows. "Okay, yes, she did try to kill me and she held Bette hostage, but she's not a liar. Somehow or another, she's got it in her head that she's entitled to it."

"I'll check that out in the morning. Your shot. Hey, how far did you get in the journals?"

I told him what I had read, and his eyes got big. "Are you kidding me? She did that? You think she spiked the lemonade? For what purpose?"

"Because she's a schemer. But what she's scheming on, I don't know. I can't understand why Calpurnia would trust Isla. How could she have been so blind?"

"That's a very good question. I guess we can both attest to the fact that sometimes you can't see what's right in front of you. Most young people weren't as sophisticated back then. Not socially, anyway. Someone like Calpurnia wouldn't know anything about the ways of the world. I suspect her cousin knew a little more."

"Hmm...a whole lot more, from what I gather."

"What's that mean?"

"Oh, nothing. Your shot!" We played until I won. "I told you pool was my game."

"I believe you!" He laughed, raising his hands like he was surrendering. I took the bottle of water he offered me. Absently, I wondered what two regular people would be doing in this situation, but we weren't two "regular" people. We were both careful and cautious, and we'd had to be—for very different reasons. Ashland had had to think about his wealth, his family name, his future. And my gift for dream catching demanded that I live a certain way. There were no sleepovers for me. I could dream what he dreamed; if those night visions were full of Detra Ann or some other woman, I would be devastated. His hand touched my cheek, and I tilted my face towards him. "Kiss me," he whispered. I nodded. He half smiled and leaned down, then kissed me like he meant it.

How weird is it that I feel like I've known this man all my life? Okay, okay. Calm down. You don't believe in that kind of stuff, do you?

When he gently pulled away, I put my arms around his neck and his went around my waist. He held me close, his head on my shoulder and mine on his chest. Finally, he let me go. We didn't say anything else, and I walked away with a smile.

I walked down the hall and through the French doors to the stepping-stone walkway. I practically hopped across each one, thrilled to be here with Ashland. I realized how lonely his life must have been. Sure, people would always be around him, but he must always wonder what they want from him. That had to be a lonely way to live.

I got ready for bed, pulling down the window shades and checking all the locks. I mean, who could jump the fence, really? The whole place was fenced, but just in case. I wanted to be safe. I slid on my pajamas, skipping my shower until morning. I know it was silly, but I just didn't want to wash his kisses away. I could still smell his cologne on my skin. I picked up my phone and texted him.

Thanks for letting me stay here tonight.

In just a few seconds, he wrote back.

My pleasure, and I can't wait to cook breakfast for you.

Sounds yummy. Goodnight.

Night, CJ.

I closed my eyes and pulled the key out of my nightgown. I stared at it and rubbed it. I thought about the house and about Calpurnia. I went to sleep praying that I would see what I wanted to see. Many hands had held this key over the years; I wondered whose hands I would see when I finally stepped into the dream, if I dreamed at all.

I thought about Ashland and what the future might hold. I thought about his beautiful face, his soft lips, his kind ways. People had no idea how kind he was....soon I was asleep and dreaming.

A pink painted fingernail spun the key on the black dining room table. The music box sat in front of her, and she slid the key into the slot. She turned, turned and turned until the music began to sing. It was a melancholy tune, one that haunted her at night, but she couldn't help herself. She could almost imagine Calpurnia singing this tune, humming it while she combed her hair or wrote in her diary.

"Mommy! Mommy!" A little boy with pink cheeks and a shock of white-blond hair ran into the room with a wooden car in his hands. "Look, Mommy! Look what my cousin gave me."

A dark-haired man smiled from the doorway. She smiled back, yet she had questions about him. Unanswered, dangerous questions. Did he really love her? Or was he only getting close to her so that he could take her son away for his own nefarious reasons? She laughed at herself. Surely, she was being paranoid about her cousin Robert. He'd never been accused of such things. It was her mind, as always, playing tricks on her.

"Mommy! Isn't it wonderful?"

"Yes! Yes, it is. Now put your car down and dance with Mommy." The little boy did as he was asked. He put the car on the table and walked back to his mother. He gave her a little bow and began to waltz with her. She laughed with delight, and he smiled up at her.

"Oh, Ashland. I love you, son."

Ashland? I woke up from the dream, sitting up straight in bed, sweating and breathing fast. That was Ashland and Emily! Poor woman. Her mind had been a fog of uncertainty—fear and curiosity. Poor Ashland—poor kid. I tried to calm my breathing and clear my mind, but it wasn't working. I decided to take a quick shower, desperate to wash away the memory of that disturbing dream. In just a few minutes, I was standing under the warm water, letting it beat down on me. Then I slid on my nightshirt and towel-dried my hair. I climbed back into the bed, purposefully banishing Ashland from my dreams. I rubbed the key and thought about Calpurnia dancing in the garden. I thought about how she felt when Muncie held her hand, how she loved to hear her mother sing those French lullabies, the ones from her childhood.

Again, I fell asleep.

Chapter 2

A smile crept across my face when I turned back to look at the pale faces watching me from behind the lace curtains of the girls' dormitory. I didn't feel sorry for any of them—all of those girls hated me. They thought they were my betters because they were orphans and I was merely the accidental result of my wealthy mother's indiscretion. I couldn't understand why they felt that way. As I told Marie Bettencourt, at least my parents were alive and wealthy. Hers were dead and in the cold, cold ground. "Worm food now, I suppose." Her big dark eyes had swollen with tears, her ugly, fat face contorting as she cried. Mrs. Bedford scolded me for my remarks, but even that did not worry me.

I had a tool much more effective than Mrs. Bedford's threats of letters to the attorney who distributed my allowance or a day without a meal. Mr. Bedford would defend me—for a price. I would have to kiss his thin, dry lips and pretend that he did not peek at my décolletage a little too long. Once he even squeezed my bosom ever so quickly with his rough hands but then pretended it had been an accident. Mr. Bedford never had the courage to lift up my skirt or ask me for a "discreet favor," as my previous chaperone had called it, but I enjoyed making him stare. It had been great fun for a month or two until I saw how easily he could be manipulated.

And now my rescuer had come at last, a man, Louis Beaumont, who claimed to be my mother's brother. I had never met Olivia, my mother. Not that I could remember, anyway, and I assumed I never would.

Louis Beaumont towered above most men, as tall as an otherworldly prince. He had beautiful blond hair that I wanted to plunge my hands into. It looked like the down of a baby duckling.

He had fair skin—so light it almost glowed—with pleasant features, even brows, thick lashes, a manly mouth. It was a shame he was so near a kin because I would have had no objections to whispering "Embrasse-moi" in his ear. Although I very much doubted Uncle Louis would have indulged my fantasy. How I loved to kiss, and to kiss one so beautiful! That would be heavenly. I had never kissed a handsome man before—I kissed the ice boy once and a farmhand, but neither of them had been handsome or good at kissing.

For three days we traveled in the coach, my uncle explaining what he wanted and how I would benefit if I followed his instructions. According to my uncle, Cousin Calpurnia needed me, or rather, needed a companion for the season. The heiress would come out this year, and a certain level of decorum was expected, including traveling with a suitable companion. "Who would be more suitable than her own cousin?" he asked me with the curl of a smile on his regal face. "Now, dearest Isla," he said, "I am counting on you to be a respectable girl. Leave all that happened before behind in Birmingham—no talking of the Bedfords or anyone else from that life. All will be well now." He patted my hand gently. "We must find Calpurnia a suitable husband, one that will give her the life she's accustomed to and deserves."

Yes, indeed. Now that this Calpurnia needed a proper companion, I had been summoned. I'd never even heard of Miss Calpurnia Cottonwood until now. Where had Uncle Louis been when I ran sobbing in a crumpled dress after falling prey to the lecherous hands of General Harper, my first guardian? Where had he been when I endured the shame and pain of my stolen maidenhead? Where? Was I not Beaumont stock and worthy *of rescue? Apparently not. I decided then and there to hate my cousin, no matter how rich she was. Still, I smiled, spreading the skirt of my purple dress neatly around me on the seat. "Yes, Uncle Louis."*

"And who knows, ma petite Cherie, perhaps we can find you a good match too. Perhaps a military man or a wealthy merchant. Would you like that?" I gave him another smile and nod before I pretended to be distracted by something out the window. My fate would be in my own hands, that much I knew. Never would I marry. I would make my own future. Calpurnia must be a pitiful, ridiculous kind of girl if she needed my help to land a "suitable" husband with all her affluence.

The coach and four turned down the red dirt road that led to the mansion. Seven Sisters, Uncle Louis had called it. Massive dark oaks lined the wide, dusty lane, so massive that I could not see the building until we were very close. When we cleared the trees, I gasped at the sheer size of the house. Seven towering columns lined the front porch, reaching up, up, up like an ancient Greek temple shining white in the glorious sun. Children and house servants scurried about to greet us, and even a couple of old hounds barked a welcome. I squealed with delight, clapping my hands. I'd never seen anything so fine in all my life. I wanted this. This was who I was, where I belonged! I was no poor relation, no orphan. I was Isla Beaumont! I deserved this kind of life, didn't I? The coach had barely stopped before I got out, excited to arrive at last.

I was disappointed that my cousin had not greeted me herself. How important was she that she could not afford to take a moment to show her "poor" cousin a kindness? When I did finally meet her, I was astonished. Taller than me by six inches, she moved with natural grace and had a quiet manner. She would never squeal with delight or misbehave as I did...as often as I could. Calpurnia was easily the prettiest girl I had ever seen, and I didn't count myself the least of those. Uncle Louis was obviously besotted with her and forgot me instantly. The two beautiful ones left this mere mortal behind, slipping away for a private chat in one of the many gardens surrounding the plantation. Again, I felt my heart harden and my hatred grow stronger. In Uncle Louis' heart, I would always be second. Well, that was no matter to me. I could play this game as well as any woman could. They did not know how smart I was, did they? I could sing, read, do figures and speak French, a little.

The servant, Hooney, didn't like me. I knew that from the moment she laid those wise, yellowed eyes on me. That made me hate her too, but I smiled as if I were as sweet as honey. It didn't do any good; she didn't tolerate foolishness, even if she was a slave. I played the game, pretending to love my cousin. But all the while, I wished she were gone from here, leaving me as the heiress. Wasn't I a Beaumont? That was far better than being a Cottonwood, surely. Perhaps I should remind Uncle Louis of that.

Hooney let me know that Christine Cottonwood did not want to see me now, that she was ill and in bed ready to have a baby. No matter to me; I hoped she would never get out of that bed. She could die there, like Marie Bettencourt's mother. "Worm food now, I suppose." I laughed at the memory.

After a few days, the newness of my surroundings began to fade, and I began to explore beyond the house. This time, no one stopped me. No one said a word to me. Where I had been a prisoner before, I now was free! I was the friend, nay, the cousin of the heiress. I was given free run of the house. Unfortunately I could not find a single man to kiss or any place where I could have fun. One day I quietly watched some of the slaves bathing in the river. I'd never seen a naked black man before. I climbed up into a live oak and nibbled on a biscuit as I watched them. I did this many times, enjoying the games they played as they splashed in the water. I wondered how shocking it would be to climb down the tree, step out of my dress and jump into the water. Would they catch me? Would they caress my white, wet skin? Would they make me their woman? I would rise out of the water like Venus emerging from the sea, my long blond hair plastered to my naked breasts. They would worship me.

Ah, only a fantasy. Even I knew that black men never touched white women—not if they wanted to live beyond the touching. Still, it must be wonderful to be had by one of these magnificent men. It was the boy Muncie who spotted me. I saw him when he did it, telling the other boys to put their clothing on. Oh, Muncie! You infuriate me! You of all people should hate Calpurnia—she is your master, your mistress. I knew he loved her in a way that he should not. I smiled at him and slithered down the tree like the snake did in the Garden. I munched on an apple and stared at the surprised boys. I took a bite and then shoved the apple into one boy's open mouth before turning and walking away. I heard them whispering behind me, some of them praying, others talking fearfully. That had not been the way I wanted that to go, but Muncie had thwarted my plans. Very well, I would hate him too!

The longer I stayed at Seven Sisters, the more people I found to hate. Reginald Ball, a cousin of Uncle Jeremiah Cottonwood, was one such person. Another man infatuated with Calpurnia, who I had decided was no great beauty after all. She had that mulatto eye color that shifted from brown to green, and her neck was far too long. I also hated Uncle Jeremiah, for he had slapped me when I tried to kiss him. I couldn't understand why he would refuse me a kiss—but when I followed him around a bit, the answer became apparent. Uncle Jeremiah had another lover—and not another woman. No, he'd chosen for himself a boy, a lovely boy with light skin, white teeth and a handsome face. His name was Early, and I believed that slave boy fancied himself in love with his Master. It made me laugh and laugh when I saw the two of them slip off into the Moonlight Garden together. What they did there was less amusing to me; I didn't care. After my spying, I'd walked back to the house smiling. The people in this house had so many secrets—secrets that would smother them. I laughed again.

I walked up the stairs to my room, wanting to think some more about this house of secrets, when I heard someone speak to me. "You seem to be enjoying your stay here." I turned on the third step, pressing my bottom against the railing, and looked into the face of a man who seemed to know me. "Have we met, sir?"

"I should think not. I have come to pay court to Calpurnia Cottonwood. But as I do not find her about, you shall do nicely."

I walked down two stairs and leveled my gaze at him. "I don't play seconds to my cousin, good sir."

"Well, had I known that you were here, I would have courted you first. How can one love a moth when such a butterfly is fluttering about?"

"You talk like you know poetry, sir. Are you a well-read man?" I stood on the step above him, and we talked in whispers now.

We talked for another hour, taking a stroll in the rose garden while Calpurnia ministered to her mother, who had taken a turn for the worse. At that first meeting, my words were careful and well-chosen. But after three such walks, we discovered that we were after the same thing—the vast riches of Calpurnia's fortune. The word was out that Christine and Louis had converted the fortune into a collection of precious jewelry pieces and that they planned to hide them from Jeremiah. The man had become a drunk and a poor manager of the Beaumont-Cottonwood estate. At least, that was what the jeweler had told Captain David Garrett while aboard the Delta Queen for a night of cards and bad behavior.

I wanted to be free, and that would take a fortune so I could live like the lady I was. David wanted to go with me; we would travel the world, first in the Bahamas, then on to Paris and then to Greece. Oh, to travel! I had kissed David impetuously in the rose garden that day, but he barely responded. His beauty attracted and stirred me as no other had. He gently pushed me away and whispered an apology, but that only made me want him more! Eventually I knew why he was so hesitant to kiss me, court me, and make love to me—because he secretly hoped that he and Calpurnia would marry. He would be the rightful heir to the fortune. I had a choice to make: stand aside or work my magic on David Garrett. If I wanted to keep him, I could. I knew enough tricks to please a man for a hundred years. But did I want him? That was the question. I couldn't make up my mind—until I saw the way Calpurnia looked at him. Her lips parted, her face tilted up, listening to his every word, her hand worrying over her intricate coiffure. Yes, it was clear she wanted him.

I went to bed smiling; now the snare could be set. I would have those jewels and David Garrett too. I had been there only a few weeks, and I already knew all about my cousin. I knew her weaknesses—those damn books of poetry, the ones that talked about love, falling in love, being in love. That's how we would do this. We would write notes; he would woo her into trusting him, and I would pass them on to her, both of us laughing at our craftiness. From time to time, he appeared to feel guilty. When I saw his resolve relaxing, I would win him over again with the tricks I'd learned with the General and his friends.

One dark night, a storm settled over Seven Sisters, and it seemed determined to tear the place down. Lightning popped around the house, snapping trees, sparking around the ponds and fountains in the Moonlight Garden. Was God punishing us for all the evil we had done? I didn't know, but I prayed for the first time in a long time. "Dear Lord, I hate Calpurnia Cottonwood. Please strike her with lightning so I alone will be the heir to the Beaumont fortune." He did not answer me, nor did my cousin die that night. Still, it did get me to thinking about the baby that Christine carried. I had heard the nurse say it was a miracle he had lasted this long; perhaps the thing would die and I wouldn't have to take care of him. I had no taste for murder, although murder had happened here, not so long ago.

Uncle Louis—beautiful, perfect Uncle Louis—was dead, buried behind the mausoleum, if those yapping dogs had not dug him up and eaten him by now. I'm sure I should feel sad about it, but I do not. Early, the slave who loved Mr. Cottonwood, had done the deed. The tall Frenchman had wandered into their trysting place (someone may or may not have told him where it was) and discovered their lovemaking. Drunk on corn whiskey, Jeremiah swore at the man but didn't do anything else. Early ran after him, his half-naked body exposed as he smashed him in the head with a garden curiosity, a concrete ball that rested atop one of the many fountains. He smashed him over and over; Uncle Louis had not made a sound from the first blow to the last. When *he was through, Early put the ball back on the fountain and the waters turned to blood. I laughed quietly at the biblical allusion from my hiding place in the maze.*

Thinking that Mr. Jeremiah had done the killing before he passed out, Stokes helped Early hide the body, burying it where it lay. "Worm food now, I suppose," I whispered to myself. "Oh no, dear Calpurnia. What can you do? Uncle Louis is gone. Who will protect you now?"

I spent the rest of the evening with Calpurnia, pretending that I had not seen a thing. We danced to the tune of the music box, and I pretended to be a doting cousin. It was an easy charade. Muncie came to serve us our dinner, and I teased him a little by asking him to join us. Calpurnia scolded me for it, but before I could make a sound against her, Stokes came in and announced that Mr. Louis' horse had returned but our uncle was missing. This news greatly alarmed Calpurnia, but I smirked. I knew! I knew what had happened! Calpurnia sent Stokes for the Sheriff and went downstairs to arrange the staff to go help look for him. It was believed at that time that he had fallen from his horse and may be in dire need of help. As the staff—even Hooney—clambered into the foyer for instructions, I silently walked towards Christine's chambers. She was asleep when I went in, but she woke up and inquired about my health. I did not offer her sweet words or hedge about my business. I began speaking in a whisper, like I was casting a spell—I told her everything that I had seen, everything I had done before I came to Seven Sisters. And when that was through, I told her what her husband was doing and who he was doing it to. I told her things you would never tell a genteel lady. I shocked her over and over again, her heart breaking with each word. She cried, but no one could hear her now that the search had started. I stood before her as she clutched the wooden bedpost, leaning against it for strength. "Louis is dead, dead, dead now. Gone. Worm food now, I suppose." That phrase had worked on Marie Bettencourt, and it worked on a fine lady like Christine Cottonwood too. She let out a heart-wrenching cry and fell to her knees holding her belly, weeping. Before I left her, I said, "You will die too now, and that baby will die. You will all be together as worm food. And when you are dead, they will put you in that cold, cold mausoleum alongside the other dead ones." She didn't answer me but stared off into space, not crying, no longer moaning, saying nothing. She finally stopped crying and sighed a little.

I squatted down beside her and held her face in my hands. I kissed her, but she was no longer with me. She stared off into the distance; her mind had closed her off from the trauma. "If you can hear me in there, Christine, don't worry. I will take care of your daughter too. You won't be alone for long." She did not respond but merely kept staring. Oh yes, this was far too easy for a girl like me, a talented girl, a girl with a future.

Chapter 3

I woke up screaming. Thankfully, no one could hear me in the guesthouse. When I realized I was awake and it had all been a dream, I put my hand over my mouth to stop myself. I had learned that trick before, to scream when I wanted the dream to end. Somehow it worked, when I remembered to do it. I got out of bed, the darkness of Isla's life weighing me down. I had seen what she had seen, done what she had done. I went to the restroom and brushed away the tastes of lemonade and gin and all those unhappy kisses. I got in the shower to wash it all away, checking my body for bruises as I scrubbed. Happily there were none. My mind rocked with all the information I had collected. When I dried off, I decided to immediately record what I had witnessed.

I flipped open my laptop and began to type like a crazed scribe. From the first moment to the last, I wrote down every thought I could remember. Now it all made sense! Oh, Captain Garrett, how could you? Calpurnia had loved you so and now, to discover it was all a ruse, it made no sense to me. I had cried more over the past couple of weeks than I had in my whole life, but I couldn't help it. My heart broke for so many of these people. I knew them. I knew even Isla in a way she would never approve of. I felt sorry for her, which she would reject immediately, but she too had been a victim at one time. Of course, she had certainly done her share of victimizing others too.

As I wrote my thoughts, feelings and dream-catching experiences, my email dinged. Once I got to a stopping place, I clicked it and was surprised to see an email from Mia's parents. My shaking finger wavered over the key for a minute before I opened the message.

Dear CJ,

I hope this letter finds you well. I was wondering, would you mind asking Mia to call us, please? We have not heard from our daughter in six months. We understand that she is busy but if you could, would you tell her? Thanks so much!

When are you coming to see us again? We miss you too!

Love,

Alice and Myron Reed

I read the email again and again. I couldn't believe what I was reading. They had no idea where their daughter was? That was heartbreaking. That meant I would be the one to deliver the bad news to them. This was so unfair! I began to type a response, but nothing came to mind. I closed the laptop and finished getting dressed. I would have to think about what I would say.

I needed to talk with Ashland about the dream. Would he believe me? He had to, didn't he? The alarm went off on my phone, reminding me that TD's Moonlight Garden presentation was that night. An involuntary shudder went through me. I packed my things and went in search of Ashland, my mind still swimming over the dream, the email and everything in between.

I found him in the kitchen, preparing breakfast as promised. I watched him quietly, waiting for the perfect time to share with him what I knew.

"Are you okay? You seem kind of quiet this morning? Trust me, I'm a great cook, and Eggs Cathedral is my specialty. Okay, it's the Spot of Tea's specialty, but I copied it."

"I had a dream last night, Ashland."

His beautiful blue eyes widened, and he set down his orange juice. "Really? Who did you dream about? I thought that only happened in historical places."

"Apparently not in Mobile. All I have to do is think about them before I go to sleep and have something they touched. It doesn't always work perfectly—I mean, sometimes you don't dream about who you intended." I thought about Ashland and his mother dancing, about her mind wandering into dark places. I decided not to tell him anything about her. I wanted to spare him that. "I intended to dream about Calpurnia, but instead I saw Isla."

"Tell me everything." He pushed his plate aside and leaned on his hands. I don't know what he expected to hear, but obviously it wasn't this. "I can't believe it. She was a psychopath or something, wasn't she? She's the reason Christine went catatonic. Oh my God!" He got up from the table and pulled his phone out of his pocket.

Sensing his mood, I panicked. "What are you doing? You can't help them—they are all gone now, Ashland."

"I'm calling TD. I am going to ask him to dig behind the mausoleum. If Louis Beaumont is there, he deserves a better resting place than that." I listened to him talk to TD. He gave a few orders but didn't tell him what he'd find. When he hung up, he said, "Beaumont might not be there anymore; no need to get TD stirred up without a reason." I didn't blame him. TD was an excitable guy, especially if he was being taken off his tight schedule. Ashland looked at me suspiciously, and it saddened me. "I don't envy you your gift, CJ. Are you okay?"

"I'm fine, Ashland. Listen, maybe I should go. I have yet another bad situation happening. Mia's parents emailed me—they haven't heard from her in months, and they want me to call them or have her call them. I've got a lot to think about. I don't want to just tell them that their daughter has lost it—that she's killed a man and tried to hurt me. What do I say?"

He just said, "Tough break. I think the best thing to do is tell the truth, no matter how hard that is."

That was easy for him to say. I cared about the Reeds and knew just how much telling them the truth would hurt. "Well, I better go. Can you give me a lift home?"

"Sure, let me get my keys." Neither one of us was in the mood for breakfast now. I knew what I had to do, and it didn't involve Ashland. "Listen, I'll be at the house in a while, but I have something to do first. I need just a few hours, if that's okay."

"Please tell me you aren't going to talk to Mia." He seemed genuinely aggravated with me. I guessed my dream had put him in a sour mood. But what was I supposed to do? I knew he didn't like my gift, but he did want my help finding Calpurnia. Didn't he?

"No, I'm not. And besides, where would I find her? I have no idea where she is." Okay, that wasn't completely true; I at least knew where I could find a lead.

By the time we reached my place, Ashland was a little more himself. He kissed me before I got out of the car, but it didn't cheer me up much. I waved at him and walked up the steps to my apartment. I liked the little place, despite the excitement of the night before. Bette's car was still gone, and I hoped she would stay away a little longer. I had something to do. I looked through my desk drawer. There it was! I held Henri Devecheaux's card and dialed the number with shaking fingers. I muttered under my breath, "What am I doing? Detective Simmons was right. I am acting like Nancy Drew." I lost my nerve and hung up. No. If I was going to do this, I was going to do it face to face. I grabbed my purse and keys. His club was on Royal Street, which wasn't that far away. Mia had mentioned that he lived in the small building next to Gabriella's. That's where I would go.

I tried not to think too much about what I was doing. I thought about Calpurnia and Isla—and what a fool Calpurnia had been. But hadn't I been a fool too? I had been blind to Mia's scheming, her jealousy of me. How odd it was to see this familiar tragedy play out again. Only this time, I was in the middle of it! I pulled onto Royal Street and stopped in front of Gabriella's. The building was closed, and all the lights were off. Obviously, it wasn't a daytime establishment. I could see a few buildings surrounding the club, but I wasn't sure which was Devecheaux's place. I wouldn't find out from here, would I? I put the car in park, got out and locked the doors behind me. I walked down the sidewalk and stood in front of an arched gate with elaborate spires on top. I pushed the gate open and walked across the brick and up the concrete steps to the big wooden door. There was a large glass window in the center. I peeked inside and saw no one, so I took a deep breath and knocked. Nothing. I knocked again. This time I heard a dog bark, a tiny dog with white fuzzy fur and a protruding lower jaw. What kind of dog was that? He was cute and ugly at the same time.

I saw Henri Devecheaux pause in the hallway. As if to say, "I'm not here to harass you," I gave him a friendly wave. He wore a gold silk robe, which he tied a little closer as he walked toward me. He opened the big door and smiled suspiciously. "Good morning, Miss Jardine. How may I help you?"

"I wanted to talk to you about Mia if you have a minute. I wouldn't bother you if it weren't urgent." I smiled nervously.

"It's no bother at all," he said in a raspy voice. "I'm sorry. I sang my heart out last night, and my voice is shot. Come on in the kitchen, and we'll talk." I followed the big man as he sashayed into a stylish kitchen decorated in a rich New Orleans style with copper pots and plenty of fleur-de-lis embellishments. "Would you like a cup of tea?"

"No, thank you."

He poured himself a cup and invited me to sit with him. "How may I help you?"

"As I mentioned, this is about Mia. She's still missing. I know the police are looking for her, but that's not why I'm here. Her parents are worried sick—they've emailed me, asking about her. Do you know where I can find her? Off the record, of course. I'm not here to spy or get you in trouble. I want to help Mia. I think she needs it." There, that was the truth.

Devecheaux took a sip from his blue teacup and set it down. He inspected me, still suspicious. "I really don't know anything, Miss Jardine."

"It's Carrie Jo, please, and any detail could help."

"She contacted me when she first came to Mobile, wanting a place to stay. She found out I was interested in the supernatural and told me I could visit the house in exchange for her staying here. I jumped at the chance, of course. Who wouldn't? Big, mysterious house, rumors of murders, interesting story. I had no idea that I wasn't supposed to be there. She told me she was the boss, and she had a key and everything. It wasn't until you broke in on us that I knew something was wrong—horribly wrong. I never meant to break the law, you know."

"I'm not here to accuse you of anything, Mr. Devecheaux."

"Please, if I'm calling you Carrie Jo, you call me Henri."

"Okay, Henri. I'm not here to accuse you of anything. I just want to find my friend."

He took the last swig of his tea and gave me a sad look. "I'm sorry, but she's not here. I think she went to stay with her musician friend, Bettencourt. They were pretty hot and heavy when she left. I wish I could tell you more. I suppose the club where he works might be able to tell you where he's at." He rubbed his baby-smooth face. "May I ask you a question? I know it's kind of personal..."

"What is it?"

"Have you had any experiences in that house?"

"What do you mean?"

"You know what I mean, Carrie Jo. Experiences, with the afterlife, ghosts, haunts—anything like that."

I stood up from the table, ready to leave. Maybe he didn't know anything after all. "I think all old houses have imprints of the past, Henri. Don't you?"

"When we were there that night, I swear there was something—someone—there. I think it was a woman or a girl. Like I say, I have an interest in these sorts of things. I have a website; would you like to see it?"

Curious, I followed him to what looked like an office or a small production studio. He walked behind a desk, and I followed him. He kicked his foot to close the bottom drawer, but not before I caught a glimpse of the music box. My heart was pounding, but I pretended to focus on the computer screen. "Oh, that is interesting," I forced myself to say. Henri Devecheaux had the music box! What did that mean? He must have believed that I missed his sleight of hand, or foot, because he began to show me the features of his website—photos, videos of supposed ghosts, links to other sites.

"So, you see, I have Oakleigh and the Bragg Mitchell Manor on here—both with their full permission, of course. They let me come in and set up my cameras, I record for twelve hours, then I publish what I find here. It's kind of a hobby. But look, I have over one hundred thousand followers. People love Old Mobile history, and they love the supernatural. It's the perfect combination for an aspiring businessman."

"That is interesting. You have done a great job with the website. A hundred thousand people? That would be great advertisement for the museum. You know, when we get it up and running."

His eyes narrowed. "That's an interesting necklace you're wearing." I hadn't realized that when I leaned forward to see his computer, the necklace with the key fell out of my shirt.

I quickly tucked it back in and smiled nervously. "Yeah, it's pretty old. Thanks for sharing your website with me. Let me talk to Ashland and see what he says. Despite what Mia told you, he is the boss." I walked toward the door without waiting. He was right behind me but hadn't tried to stop me so far. "Thank you for your help, Henri. I hope I can get Mia the help she needs."

He smiled as he opened the door, but it didn't give me any comfort. I stepped out, feeling safer by the second but not by much. He said, "If I were you, Carrie Jo, I would leave that girl alone. She's not all there, and she sure doesn't consider you her friend anymore. She's obsessed with you, with that house and with...well, let's say she's a girl of many interests."

"Thank you. I will remember that." I walked down the steps as quickly as I could. My hands shook as I got into the car. This was too much! Devecheaux had the music box. I could see him watching from the doorway. I wanted to call Ashland, but I had to get out of there! I drove like a madwoman to Seven Sisters.

There were only a few work trucks on the property. The unveiling of the Moonlight Garden was that night, and it was going to be a small affair, mostly for the team and a few other folks. To my surprise, Detra Ann was there, talking with Ashland and TD. The brunette seemed about as happy to see me as I was to see her.

"Ashland, I have to talk to you."

"Okay, sure. Let's go out back. I have to tell you something anyway." We walked down the long hallway to the back door. This was the very hallway where Ashland had seen Isla as a child and she'd kissed him. "Listen, I told TD to hold off on digging right now. I was thinking that Louis Beaumont has rested this long, and one more night isn't going to hurt. And we've got people from the Historical Society coming to this tonight. It's not unusual to find skeletons on an old property like this, but not usually when the locals are visiting. What do you think?"

"Ashland, I found the music box. It's at Henri Devecheaux's."

"What? Really? That's where you went this morning? Why didn't you tell me? I would have gone with you. Do you know how much danger you put yourself in?" He ran his hand through his hair, and his jaw popped tensely. *Was he angry with me? When I was trying to help him?*

"I'm fine! I'm telling you I saw the music box—but I didn't get it. It was in a drawer in Devecheaux's office. And I think he saw this..." I showed him the key on my necklace.

"That's it! We've got to call Detective Simmons and tell her what you found out. Someone has to protect you!" He slid his phone out of his pocket.

"No, we can't do that! You said you wanted to wait on exhuming Beaumont's remains because you didn't need the bad publicity right now, but won't calling Simmons in to get the necklace do the same thing? I don't think Devecheaux knows I saw the box, so we should be okay. Let's wait until tomorrow and take care of all this nasty business at once. I'd hate to see TD's big night ruined."

"You're probably right, but I'm not happy about it. And I'm not happy you went over there alone to confront that man. He's twice your size, Carrie Jo. What would have happened if he had decided to take that necklace from you? You couldn't have stopped him."

"He didn't, and I'm fine. Stop worrying. We have a party to prepare for, don't we?"

"I don't think you and I have much to do. Detra Ann and TD seem to have everything covered. Let's get out of here a while. I'm starving—I missed my breakfast because an obsessed historian wanted to go play Sherlock Holmes. What am I going to do with you, CJ?"

"I don't know. Kiss me again?"

Chapter 4

That afternoon, I made it a point to buy a white dress. It was the one request TD had made: everyone was to wear white—I guess so we'd all "glow" in the dark. I wasn't a shopper. I liked buying online, but there was no time for that. In the end, I had to go to Hermes Bridal. I found a dress I loved; it was sleeveless with beadwork and a fringed hem. It was kind of a flapper style, and I thought it was perfect for a summer garden party. It had a steep price tag, but it was worth it. I looked wonderful in it.

As I shopped for shoes, I thought about my brunch with Ashland. We'd stopped by Bienville Tea Emporium and ordered mimosas and some of the best food, apart from Bette's, that I had ever tasted. It was nice to be in the moment, not stuck in the past. So much sadness there. The past is where all the regrets go. Regrets don't live in the present—they always trail behind you, tap you on the shoulder and say, "Remember me?" I didn't want to live a life of regrets. I wanted to always think of the present moment. I couldn't do anything about my dream life, but after spending a significant amount of time in Isla's "skin," I knew how dangerous that could be. Always thinking of the past. Counting regrets. Using pain as fuel for life. So toxic and deadly. How easy it would be to do just that.

At nine o'clock, I drove to the house, pulling in behind Ashland's sleek Mercedes. My Honda looked out of place, even with four new tires, but here I was. It was pitch black out, and I could see the moon rising high above us. No clouds, no hint of rain. It was the perfect night for this, I supposed, even though Louis Beaumont's body was probably just on the other side of the maze, behind the Cottonwood Mausoleum. A shiver ran down my spine. I remembered the first time I walked up this sidewalk, the first time I stood before the columned porch of the house. How different it looked now, yet so much the same. The painted white columns looked almost blue in the moonlight. Two newly installed gas lamps flickered at the bottom of the steps, lighting the way for visitors to the great mansion. Thankfully, the satyr fountain, an addition that had arrived sometime at the turn of the century, had been relocated somewhere less frightening and offensive. I couldn't have been happier about that decision.

Light poured through the windows, and soft music played, the piano player warming up for the soiree. What had begun as a small event for the team had somehow evolved into a party of fifty, complete with live music, champagne and appetizers. I knew who I could thank for that—Detra Ann. *What's your problem, CJ? You're jealous of nothing. She and Ashland are just friends. Come on now, be nice.* I wasn't normally a jealous person, but I couldn't deny what I felt. It was this house, I reasoned, feeling the cold chills shimmy down my spine.

Speak of the devil, it was Detra Ann who greeted me at the door. "Hi, Carrie Jo! You look great! I think Ashland is in the Blue Room."

I smiled, determined to overcome my own pettiness. Tall and athletic, Detra Ann was a pretty woman, and the white handkerchief dress she'd chosen showed off her toned curves and exquisite tan. I strode to the Blue Room, where I found Ashland sliding a box on my desk.

He turned around when he heard me come in. "Hi! Wow, you look great!"

"You sound surprised," I teased him.

"Nothing you do surprises me. Remember the first night we met? You fell in my arms?"

"That's not how I remember it. I fell on my head—you carried me in your arms." I stood on tiptoe and kissed him. "What's that?"

"A delivery for you, but that can wait. Let's go find TD and let him know we're here. According to Detra Ann, he's a nervous wreck. You know, I think those two might have something going on."

I raised an eyebrow. "Really? Well, she's done a great job decorating for the party. I think maybe we should think about having that Christmas ball after all—if you're still interested. Might be fun."

He smiled and said, "Let's wait and see how many more bodies turn up around here. We may not be able to get anyone here for a ball, except a few ghosts."

"Don't say that." I was dead serious. The ghosts of the past were always listening. "Please."

"Okay, okay. Come on, I need a drink or two. Let's put on our happy faces."

We found our way to the bar that had been set up in the ladies' parlor. The two Rachels, their dates, James, Chip and Chip's mom were already there. I hugged everyone's neck, and Ashland and I posed for photos with our group. We wandered around, talking to the visitors and sharing stories about the renovation process. One thing I could say about Mobile was that it was full of interesting characters—that included the wealthy and elite of local society.

At ten o'clock, TD finally appeared, welcoming us to the opening of the Moonlight Garden. He gave a brief history lesson on how the garden worked and then pulled aside the heavy dark curtains that covered the back doors. He and Detra Ann opened the doors, and the sight was nothing short of amazing. Moonlight bounced off the statues, the white flowers, the bleached walkways. I caught my breath at how perfectly TD had managed to recreate the garden that I knew from my dreams. I held onto Ashland's arm; he looked down at me, searching my face, but I nodded at him. "I'm okay," I whispered. The hedges were intact, although not as tall as they had been, and a few of the large trees were missing, but everything else was in place. I walked down the back steps and stood on the pathway. I could close my eyes and completely believe that Muncie or Calpurnia was very near to me.

"Ladies and gentlemen, I present the Moonlight Garden. Please take a tour and enjoy the grounds. Detra Ann has kindly provided a basket of flashlights if you need extra lighting. I'll be here if you have any questions."

The excited gathering filled the garden, some taking flashlights but most opting for the "natural" tour. It was a sight to behold. "TD, you have done a wonderful job. You can't possibly know how accurate this is to the original. It is simply breathtaking."

He hugged me and shook Ashland's hand. "Thank you for allowing me to be part of this. This has been a real labor of love. Now go take the tour and tell me what you think."

I wiped a tear or two from my eye, chose not to take a flashlight, and walked into the Moonlight Garden with Ashland. The house disappeared behind us, swallowed up by the massive gardenias that TD had so carefully planted and manicured. It was as if they had been here all along, hiding, waiting to be recognized again. The garden path veered to the right from the entrance, leading visitors along the hedgerow, where it turned to the left. I didn't need anyone to tell me where to go, because I'd already been here. The path led from statue to statue to the back of the property. I looked up at Ashland, and his blond hair made him look like one of the statues shining in the moonlight. His dazzling smile only added to the effect.

Suddenly a scream filled the garden, and Ashland and I rushed toward the sound. We didn't have far to go. Chip's mother lay on the ground, her flashlight beside her. The skinny young man with the oversized glasses tried to help her up, but she screamed again.

"No, let me sit for a minute, boy, or I might hurt myself worse. Oh, my ankle!" Chip shrugged and stood helplessly over his mother.

Ashland squatted down beside her. "Are you okay? Should I call an ambulance?"

She smiled, and her hand fluttered to her neck. "Oh no, I'm sure I will be okay. Maybe you could help me up? I just need to get off this ankle. I stepped wrong, is all. I won't sue you or anything," she said with a giggle, putting her arms around Ashland's neck. "Wait a minute. You're Ashland Stuart, aren't you? I thought that was you. I'm Arnette, Chip's mother."

"Nice to meet you, Arnette. Let me help you up." Ashland and Chip awkwardly got her to her feet, and she held onto both of them.

"I just need to rest. Oh, oh, it hurts."

I smiled at Ashland. He had his hands full, and I was more than happy to let him handle it. "I'll see you in a few," I said. I hated that we wouldn't be walking through the garden together, but I felt compelled to continue the tour. I could hear the others laughing and joking about the dark, and someone even howled at the moon. I walked on, passing first Alcyone, the statue of the sister who was seduced by Poseidon. Next came Sterope, who had been ravished by Ares, then Celaeno, Electra, Merope and Maia, each statue representing in some way the tragic figures of the Pleiades or the Seven Sisters. Finally, the path took me to Taygete, the last of the statues before the Atlas fountain, and to me the sweetest. Taygete had a long, graceful neck and elegant arms that she waved above her head. Her foot was placed on the back of a deer's head, a hind sent by Artemis to wing her away from Zeus' unwanted advances. Around Taygete grew a myriad of white flowers. I plucked one from a bush; it looked like a star. Some species I didn't recognize, but I saw some flowers that I did know: the Oxeye Daisy, Hepatica, devil's trumpets. I also noticed that TD had placed mirrors about the garden to bounce the light around, creating an unexpected glowing effect. Taygete's feet flowed in the dark like an unearthly spotlight. In my dreams, the garden was much darker, but this was lovely beyond words. I felt as if I had stepped right into another world. I stared at Taygete again, wishing Ashland could be here, when suddenly I got the feeling I was being watched. I wasn't alone in the garden anymore.

Creak, creak, creak. I froze after getting to my feet, the flowers in my hand. *Creak, creak, creak.* "Who's there? Is that you, Rachel? Detra Ann?" Nobody answered me. The garden was so quiet that even the crickets had stopped chirping. It was as if I had entered a vacuum. I didn't hear the voices of the partiers, and even the moon seemed different. I stepped into a clearing, feeling disoriented and slightly nauseated. *Must be the champagne. I must have had too much.* I leaned against the Taygete statue, trying in vain to catch my breath.

Then I saw her—standing in the moonlight, in the gap between the two hedges. I blinked, staring into the night, still shocked by what I saw. It was Isla, stone-faced, her hands folded in front of her in her skirt. She saw me but said nothing, just backed away without turning, disappearing into the hedge. My first thought was, "Run! Run now!" but I heard the sound again. *Creak, creak.* I had to know what I was hearing. The white flowers slid from my hand, and I stepped as quietly as I could down the path to the spot where she'd disappeared. Suddenly I saw a gap in the hedge, which I was sure had not been there before. I held my breath and stepped across into another small clearing. An old oak tree towered above the clearing, preventing the moonlight from falling fully on the ground below. Instead, it shone in splotches, here and there. Under the tree, a rope swing with an old board for a bottom swung back and forth as if someone had just leaped out of it. I walked to it, stilling it with my hands, the old ropes creaking as I did. That was the sound I'd heard. I touched the wood; it felt real. *This was real, right?* Again my senses were pricked by the feeling that someone was watching me.

Isla stood behind me. I knew without looking. I turned slowly, trying to prepare my mind for what I was about to see. It didn't do me any good. She was about six feet from me, looking as real as anyone I had ever seen. Her hair was carefully curled and pinned up, spirals of golden hair dangled, covering her ears. A green jade necklace hung at her neck, and she wore a black and grey dress with billowing sleeves. Her young face stared back at me; it appeared twisted with anger, her fury ready to be released upon me. I was not wanted here! A breeze began to blow through the clearing, a swirl of air that tossed flower petals to the ground and moved the heavy tree limbs as if they were touched by giants. The air became wintry. Isla suddenly smiled, turned and stretched out her arms, welcoming an invisible stranger to her secret garden. As he came closer, a faint image appeared, the outline of a man. His long, dark hair and white collared shirt were unmistakable—it was David Garrett. He was heartbreakingly handsome in a storybook sort of way. He whispered in Isla's ear like a caring lover would, playfully touching her curls. He smiled down at her and slid his arm around her small waist, and the two walked away to the entrance of the clearing. The captain was fully visible now but still unaware of my presence. Before the couple disappeared, the girl looked back at me with a bottomless stare. I stood by the swing, closing my eyes to avoid seeing everything swirl into blackness.

I woke with Ashland on his knees next to me. The Taygete statue towered above me, and the evening was warm and balmy.

No more coldness—no more Isla. "What happened?" I asked him.

He laughed nervously. "I could ask you the same thing. Did you fall or decide this was a good place to take a nap?"

"No." I sat up, shaking my head. I felt okay, no bangs or bruises, as far as I could tell. "I walked through the clearing over there and woke up here."

"What clearing?"

"The one over there." I stood, knocking the fallen flowers from my skirt. I walked to the hedge, but the opening was now gone. My guess was it had never been there, at least not in recent years.

"What happened, CJ? Did you see something?" His eyes searched mine. I hated seeing that desperate look on his handsome face. He had looked up at his mother like that, wanting to rescue her, save her. I didn't want that. At that moment, I wanted him to see me as normal—I wanted to *be* normal. Maybe I would tell him later, but not now. He'd had enough for one day.

"I don't know, really, but I feel fine now. Can we go back to the house?"

He nodded. I knew he didn't believe me, but he was enough of a gentleman not to press me. We walked back holding hands. Once in a while, I couldn't help but look back. I didn't see anyone other than the invited, living guests.

"Let me get you some water."

I smiled at him. "That sounds great. I'll be hiding out in the Blue Room for a few minutes."

He laughed, and I strolled down the hall, closing the double doors behind me. I leaned against the cool painted wooden doors. What had this house done to me? Did I really want to stay here? How much more could I see? How much more could I take? I sighed and walked to my desk. There was the forgotten box. I read the return address—it was from H. Devecheaux. I reached for the letter opener and cut through the tape. On top of a wad of tissue paper was a note.

Dearest Miss Jardine,

I humbly ask your forgiveness for my involvement with Mia Reed and her schemes. I am returning this music box to you in hopes that, in some way, doing this might make amends. She left this item with me when she moved and asked me to keep it for her. Even though I didn't want to, I did as she asked because Mia can be a dangerous, demanding woman.

I cannot tell you how I worry for you, as Mia thinks of nothing else but reclaiming a lost treasure that she is convinced you are keeping from her. Please be aware that she is a danger to you and to anyone who stands in her way.

As for my part, I regret the night at Seven Sisters. I regret calling up those old ghosts, for ever since that night, I have not had a decent night's sleep. I cannot shake the feeling that I am being watched and that death hangs close to me. Perhaps when this box is returned, I shall finally have some peace. I am leaving Mobile. I do not plan to return. Please express my sincere apologies to Mr. Stuart, Detective Simmons and everyone else I have hurt.

Yours,

Henri Devecheaux

I tossed the tissue and note aside and stared at the delicate-looking music box. My hands shook as I removed it from the box. I set it on my desk and slipped the necklace off my neck. Somewhere on this box was a hidden keyhole, the keyhole that operated not only the music but also a hidden compartment. Again I felt that someone was watching me. I rubbed my fingers over the enamel figurines, the dancing couple caught forever in a waltz. At the base of the podium that held the couple, I spotted a smooth piece of brass. I carefully slid the brass piece away. The hinge moved easily; someone else had found the spot recently but could get nowhere without a key. With shaking hands, I slid the key into the slot and turned it, hearing it click. The top of the box opened up to reveal a bright red, velvet-lined interior. Inside was a folded slip of paper. With trembling hands, I removed it without unfolding it. The lettering on the outside was perfect, like someone had written it yesterday.

"Here's your water...is that the box?" Ashland's face went white, and he froze.

I nodded up at him. "I found the compartment. It was in the base, and I found this note there. Ashland, I think you should be the one to read it. I suspect it is from Christine."

He put the water on the desk and accepted the note. He carefully unfolded the stiff paper, spreading it out on the table in front of me. "No, let's read it together."

Dearest Daughter,
Find your True Self, and you will Find a Treasure!
All my Deepest Love,
Christine Beaumont Cottonwood

I blinked, staring at the page. *True self, true self. Where had I seen that before?*

"This is impossible. I don't get that at all. What does this mean? Was she out of her head when she wrote this?" Ashland's discouragement didn't bother me. I was a historian—solving mysteries was my job.

I frowned at him. "Let's think about this for a minute. It's a riddle meant to confuse anyone who doesn't have any business reading it. Like you and me. Wait a second. You read most of that diary, didn't you? How did Calpurnia always describe herself? Her true self. She was a girl who liked literature. She would have identified with a heroine, a character, maybe even a... oh my gosh!"

"What is it, CJ?"

"Her neck, she hated her neck. Even Isla mentioned that Calpurnia had a long neck. That's it!" I stood up quickly from the desk, the rolling desk chair flying away awkwardly. I know where it's at!"

"Are you serious?"

I grinned and nodded, as excited as a kid running to the ice cream truck. "We will need a shovel, though."

"A shovel? If this requires digging anywhere around here, we'd better wait until after the party. Only thirty more minutes. Can you wait that long?"

I pretended to bite a fingernail. "I can if you can."

Chapter 5

What would Detective Simmons think about Ashland and me digging in the garden of Seven Sisters on a moonlit night? She'd probably raise a ginger brow, lick the lead of her pencil and waste no time whipping out her notebook. Yet here we were, dressed in white like two ghosts, slinging dirt from a hole we dug in front of the Taygete statue. We'd been digging for ten minutes—the adrenaline was beginning to wear off now, and I was starting to worry that my hunch had been wrong. Dead wrong. That nagging voice in my heart that only spoke when something was going horribly wrong began whispering in my ear. *I can't believe you didn't take the time to do some research first!*

I leaned against the shovel, trying to catch my breath. The sweat that covered my face and neck was like sweet nectar for an irritating chorus of Alabama mosquitoes. They apparently couldn't resist it. It didn't matter that it was coming up on midnight. It was still hot out. "Ashland, maybe we should come back in the daytime, bring a metal detector or something."

"Are you saying you were wrong? Could we be looking in the wrong place?" He leaned on the rusty handle of his shovel.

I frowned. "No, I don't think I'm wrong, but I want to be absolutely sure before we tear up all of TD's work."

"That only seems fair!" Ashland and I looked up to see our contractor, Terrence Dale, standing just a few feet away. He watched us with his hands on his hips, a cross between amused and aggravated. "May I ask what the hell y'all are doing? Ashland, I know I just work for you, but this was my project.

Why are you digging holes in the...." A sudden realization hit him. He knew what was happening. "What exactly are you looking for?"

Ashland gave him an apologetic smile. "Sorry, TD. We didn't want to do this in front of you. I know this sounds ridiculous, but Carrie Jo thinks she knows where the Cottonwood treasure is located. We have good reason to believe that it's here, under or around the Taygete statue. I promise I'll get the garden looking like it's supposed to again if it takes me all week."

"Why here?"

I swatted away mosquitoes and explained to him what I knew: in some of Calpurnia's journals she referred to herself as T, which I believed stood for Taygete. I repeated her mother's clue, *Find your True Self, and you will Find a Treasure.* Taygete was Calpurnia's "true self." She was a character that Calpurnia identified with, a doomed young woman with a long neck and an unkind father.

"That makes sense, but I hate to tell you this—I moved the Taygete statue. It was over there," he said as he pointed to an old hedge, "but to me it made more sense to put it here instead, more like the star alignment."

"So you're telling me we're digging in the wrong place?" I panted, tossing aside another shovelful of dirt.

"That's what I'm telling you. The original location was in there." He pointed beyond the massive hedge, where I had seen Isla Beaumont meet Captain David Garrett. There had been a swing and maybe a statue or a fountain; I had not been paying attention—my eyes had been fixed on the ghost of Calpurnia's cousin as she waited for her lover. She hadn't wanted me there, that much I knew. I felt her presence again, on the edge of the garden, approaching slowly to see what the interlopers were up to. Maybe I was imagining things. I wasn't a psychic—just a dreamer.

I shuddered and thought of that old southern saying the old-timers used when hit with a sudden case of chills, *A rabbit ran over my grave!*

"Come on," TD said. "If you're determined to look for something, don't tear up the entire place. That hedge is pretty old, but if we go around to the other side, I can show you how to get in there." We followed him through the thick bushes, forcing our way into the hidden clearing.

There I was again—only this time I hadn't slipped through a supernatural door. Only a broken stump of the old tree remained; the statue was gone, and no swing hung from the branches. *I had touched that swing! I heard it creak, right?* There was no scent of magnolias, just the heavy odor of dead leaves and dirt. I could feel her even closer. "Ashland, we're not alone here." I was talking about Isla, but that was before I saw someone step into the secret garden with us—it was Henri Devecheaux.

"What are you doing here, Mr. Devecheaux?"

His eyes were wide with fear as he stared at me. He didn't say anything, then suddenly let loose a blood-curdling howl and fell to the ground as if he were dead. I tossed down the shovel and ran toward him.

Devecheaux lay like a dead man on the thick green grass of the Moonlight Garden, but it was clear he was very much alive. His dark pupils were encircled with white, staring up into the vastness of the starry Alabama sky. Crouching near him, I put my head on his chest just to be sure—his heart was slow but steady.

"We need to get him to a hospital, but I'm afraid to move him!"

Suddenly the leaves in the garden shook loose from the oaks and magnolias that encircled the hidden clearing, pelting us with flowers and painful seed pods. The silky magnolia blooms blanketed everything with an unearthly white glow. I cleared the flowers off of Devecheaux's face and said, "Mr. Devecheaux! Henri! What happened? Why are you here?"

Through clenched teeth he said, "She's coming!"

"What? Who's coming?" Ashland's blue eyes were wide, and his hands shook. He got on his feet and looked around, unable to detect the intruder. But I had no doubt who was coming—and why.

"We've got to find that treasure. It's the only way to stop her!" I shouted at him over the sounds of rustling leaves and breaking tree limbs. My heart pounded in my chest, and I could hear an eerie buzzing in my ears like a hundred voices trying to speak at once. I let out a little sob but bit my lip, refusing to let fear paralyze me.

"CJ! We have to get him out of here!" Ashland held his hand up to his face, trying to protect himself from a barrage of heavy foliage.

"She's not going to let us—we have to find the treasure, now!" I turned to TD, who appeared as frozen as the statue. He seemed completely unable to process what was happening. I felt sorry for him, but there was no time to explain. "TD! We have to dig! We have to find whatever it is that's buried here. Please help me!"

Digging into the ground like a madwoman, I tossed dirt as quickly as I could. This was a long shot, wasn't it? How would we know where to dig? I had to go on blind faith, praying silently, hoping that God was listening and willing to help us.

TD shouted, "Over here! I think I hit something!"

Just as suddenly as it had started, the blowing leaves stopped. Everything went completely still, and the air around us took on a honey hue, just like when I had walked into the clearing before. I looked at the spot where the opening had appeared in the hedge, and there she was—Isla. "Ashland, get over here! Now!" I pointed at the phantom visitor, screaming at the top of my lungs.

Ashland looked and then scrambled to his feet, dragging the big man with him. Isla hovered above the ground, and the edges of her dress hem faded into the grass. She wore a blue gown, and her hair fell in perfect ringlets across her shoulders. Her eyes were on me, full of ferocious hate. TD had stopped his digging; even he could see the ghost watching us. "For God's sake, TD! Keep going!" I shouted. I ran to his side and began helping him pry a small wooden box out of the ground. I forced my shovel blade into the dirt, grunting with the effort, and eased the box up. TD reached down and grabbed it, brushing the dirt off. The lid had elaborate fasteners and a metal nameplate. He rubbed at it and read aloud, "CBC!"

"Christine Beaumont Cottonwood!" I took the box and held it tightly. I wanted to open it, but I knew I shouldn't. This wasn't my task—Ashland had to do it. He had to claim what was his, what had rightfully been Calpurnia's. That was the only way to break Isla's claim on the thing she'd wanted so badly. She'd plotted and schemed for the treasure, willing to destroy whomever or whatever got in her way. Even death had not stopped her hate for her cousin.

Ashland and Devecheaux stumbled toward us, and Isla glided behind them unblinking. I helped Devecheaux sit on the ground; his breathing was fast, and I imagined his heart pounded in his chest as mine did. All of a sudden, she stopped and raised her face so we could see her fully. Her skin was gray, her lips bloodless, her eyes dark, not blue as they had been in life. She extended a hand to Ashland, giving him a dead smile, an invitation to...something. A kiss? To think that face had charmed Captain Garrett into doing the unthinkable. Ashland took a step back, almost walking into the hole before TD stopped him.

"Ashland," I said, "you have to open the box, now!" I passed the dirty container to him.

Isla ignored me, her skin no longer gray but vibrant. I caught my breath at how alive and beautiful she appeared; except for the faded hem and invisible shoes, you would have sworn that she indeed lived and breathed. She gave him a sweet smile and slid closer. "Darling," she whispered.

"Ashland! Don't look at her. Open the box!"

He tried to work the latch, but his fingers wouldn't cooperate. "It's locked!"

"Bang it with a shovel or something!" TD yelled at us desperately.

"No, wait. Try this!" I slid the necklace from around my neck. It had fit the lock in the music box, so maybe it would work here too. Ashland took the key and slid it into the rusty lock. At first it refused to open. Isla inched forward again, just a few feet from us now. The soft, yielding look was gone from her face, and her jaw was tight. That soulless buzzing filled my ears again. Ashland jiggled the lock, and the lid opened. He pulled a velvet bag out and let the box fall to the ground. I grabbed his hand, and together we stood holding Christine's lost treasure.

"Is that what you want, Isla? You can't have it! It doesn't belong to you—it never did! This belongs to me and Calpurnia—not you, never you! Now leave us—leave Seven Sisters! You have no claim here anymore!" he shouted at her.

Her face contorted into a scream, but no sound came. Her skin faded to gray again, her blue eyes turned black, then gray, and the bright yellow color seeped from her hair. She didn't flee but simply faded into nothingness, taking all the warmth from the air around us. She was there, and then she wasn't. The buzzing stopped, and the air was still. The honey hue had changed back to muggy darkness.

"She's gone," I said. "She's gone." I smiled with relief, but it faded when I looked at Ashland. He was as white as his shirt. TD was on his knees near the hole he'd dug, and Devecheaux lay on the ground, now truly like a dead man.

I prayed that he wasn't.

Chapter 6

Ashland and I trailed the ambulance all the way to Springhill Memorial Hospital. Neither of us spoke during the frantic car ride. We were too busy trying to navigate the traffic. The clinking of the flashers was the only sound. *Did that really happen? Did we just experience the supernatural? Had we really found a treasure?* My dirt-stained dress and my dirty legs and fingers all attested to that.

Even though Ashland was dirty from head to toe too, his blond hair glowed in the moonlight. His hair was quite like Louis Beaumont's, but Ashland was tan. He was not the tall, luminous figure that his great-uncle (times eleven?) had been. The Stuart blood ran strong in him too.

Yes, it had happened. The black velvet pouch lay tossed in the backseat, untouched and unopened. Ashland swung behind the emergency vehicle as it parked. "I'm going to park around here somewhere. Why don't you walk in with Devecheaux? I'll meet you inside."

"Okay." I stepped out of the car and watched him drive away. The hospital workers lifted the gurney out of the back of the ambulance. There was the big man wrapped in white sheets, trying to talk but only mumbling.

"We're sorry, sir. We can't hear you. Who's that? Who are you looking for? Someone named... No, I can't understand. It's okay, Mister...."

"His name is Henri. It's Henri Devecheaux."

"You a family member? Wife? Girlfriend?"

"No, just a friend. He came to my party tonight. Is he going to be okay?" I attempted to follow him into triage but was blocked by an unsympathetic nurse.

"Ma'am, you'll have to wait until the doctor assesses him. Why don't you follow me, and we'll fill out his paperwork. Do you know if he has insurance?"

"No, but since he had his heart attack or stroke or whatever this is on the property of Seven Sisters, I'm sure my boss will want to cover the hospital bills. I can give you that information easily."

"That sure is nice of your boss. Who are you working for?"

"I work for Ashland Stuart, the owner of Seven Sisters. We had a garden party tonight."

"Huh. I didn't know anyone was living there."

"Not living there—just a party. It's kind of a museum now." Answering all these questions was aggravating, but I had to keep my cool.

"Let me look at you. Are you injured?" She appraised my outfit with an unbelieving eye. "You sure you two weren't in a wreck?"

What was I going to tell her? That we'd done war with a ghost? "I'm fine. And yes, I am very sure. No wreck."

She raised her ultra-thin eyebrows but didn't challenge me. It certainly didn't help that Ashland walked up completely filthy too. "Yeah, I'm sure y'all had quite the party over there at that big house."

She left, disappearing behind the door of the triage room. After about fifteen minutes, it was clear she was in no hurry to come back. I whispered, "Nobody can know what happened in the Moonlight Garden tonight. Who would believe it, Ashland?"

"They'll just have to believe it. I know what I saw—it was Isla there. We all saw her. I think she wanted me to kiss her or help her or...I don't know. It's weird because I knew what she was trying to do. Isla wanted to trick me into taking her place. Somehow, I knew that. Could you feel that? Like you said, though, when I pulled the bag out of the box, it was all over with."

As he spoke, I began to feel the same kind of "wrongness" I had felt in the garden. Not nearly as strong, but there it was. Hoping, looking for a way back in. I knew what we had to do. "Oh my goodness, Ashland. This feels wrong. There's still a chance something...that she could.... You've got to look at it—to see it." I was almost in tears. "You need to touch it, take possession of it. Let's go now. Follow me. You do have it with you, right?"

He nodded, wide-eyed, and followed me to the ladies' room. I checked the stall—no one was inside. We were alone. I locked the door and stared at us in the mirror. No wonder the nurse thought I was crazy. I was covered in dirt from head to toe. I wanted to wash my face, but more than anything, I wanted to look inside the pouch. What treasure could be so precious that a soul would defy Death to retrieve it?

Isla had not been clever enough to solve the riddle herself during her lifetime. Poor Callie didn't even know about it, really. The young heiress hadn't discovered that the box held a clue, a precious clue that would eventually lead us to the right spot to unearth the hidden prize. Now here we were—dirty and disheveled, hiding in the ladies' room on the ER floor of Springhill Memorial Hospital. At least the bathroom was clean.

"Are you ready to look?" I whispered to him hurriedly.

"Definitely. Let's see what all this has been about."

I heard a soft buzz again, but Ashland didn't react. I must have been the only one who heard it, but I knew she was lurking about, watching.

He pulled on the strings of the dry-rotted bag, loosening them with shaking fingers. Without looking inside, he plunged his hand into the bag and removed a heavy necklace loaded with sapphires set in gold and silver. Their brilliance had not lessened with time. I held my breath as he passed them to me, thinking of who must have held them last. Had it been Christine Cottonwood or Louis Beaumont? Or perhaps someone else? Carefully, Ashland dumped the remaining contents into his hands. There were ten gold coins, the likes of which I'd never seen, two sapphire earrings encrusted with diamonds, gold and silver, and lastly a bracelet with hundreds of diamonds shining brightly under the fluorescent light.

The bad feeling began to fade slowly, and then she was gone. She'd seen that we'd found her treasure, or what she had believed was hers. She had seen, and now she was gone. I prayed that I would never see or feel her again.

Someone knocked on the door, and we quickly stuffed the items back into the bag. Ashland put it in his pocket, and we went to the sink to clean up. We scrubbed up with soap and water, washing our arms and faces. The knocking persisted. "Just a minute, please," I called to our impatient visitor.

Once we'd finished our "birdbath," we walked out together, our heads held high. We'd done nothing wrong. Let her think whatever she wanted.

"You found the treasure, and the spell is broken, Ashland. She's gone. Can't you feel it?"

He smiled sadly. "Yes, but tomorrow, I will have to answer some questions. People are going to want to know how I found these and where."

"So you'll tell them. No biggie. Just don't tell them the supernatural stuff. People don't believe in that, you know."

"Yes, I do know." He still looked sad, obviously remembering that he had been one of those people just the day before.

"Are you worried about Mr. Devecheaux?" I asked. "I'm sure he will be okay now that he's here."

"I need to check in with TD. He didn't take any of this well at all. He'd been so adamant about the house not being haunted. Definitely a nonbeliever in the supernatural, and now his world has been rocked. I'm sure he'll have some questions, and I hope I can answer them." With a thoughtful look, he added, "I'm thinking of Uncle Louis too, murdered and buried in an unmarked grave. I have to correct that. To think, Isla knew what happened to him but refused to tell anyone. What kind of sick family do I come from?"

"Not sick. Just a family with secrets. They just kept too many secrets. Let's go see Mr. Devecheaux."

"Shouldn't we wait until they call us?" he asked, his hand on his pocket protectively.

"Hell no! You're Ashland Stuart, for goodness sake. Use your clout for once. Pull some strings. Get us back there!"

He grinned. "You're right. Be back in a minute." And in just five minutes, he was back with a big smile on his face. "Come on, I'll take you to his room."

"He has a room already?"

"He does now. He's up on the third floor. Here's the elevator."

I smiled at him, put my arms around his neck and hugged him. "We found the treasure, and now we have to find Calpurnia. I promised you I would, and I mean it. We will find her and bring her home."

"The more I think about it, the more I wonder if that's what she would want. She spent so much time trying to escape Seven Sisters; it might be too ironic, too cruel to bring her back here. If she ever left. Still, I want to know where she is—what happened to her. Did Isla know that too? Someone knows. She deserves to be found, CJ. I'm glad that you're committed to this. Tell me...is life always like this with you?"

I thought of what Isla had said in my dream: *Worm food now, I suppose.* What had happened to the enchanting girl with the elegant neck, beautiful hair and unassuming, sometimes nervous smile? "No, my life was pretty normal, minus the occasional dream, until I met you. Or maybe it's the house? Maybe it's Seven Sisters that's bringing all this out."

We stepped off the elevator and onto the third floor, which was apparently the cardiac unit. The doctors must have thought Devecheaux had indeed had some type of cardiac event. That didn't bode well. *Please, God, help him.*

I hoped He would listen. We pushed the door open to find Devecheaux quite alone. The mocha-skinned man's only companions were some noisy machines that dinged every so often. I walked softly to his bedside and held his hand. "Mr. Devecheaux. Henri. Can you hear me?"

At first he didn't respond, but I tried again. "Henri, can you hear me? It's me, CJ. And Ashland is here too."

He opened his eyes and looked at me. I saw a tear slide down his cheek. "You're okay," he whispered, then looked at Ashland. "And you're okay. Thank you, Lord."

"Yes, we're fine. What about you? What does the doctor say, Henri?"

"I don't know. I can't remember. But you are okay, so that's all that matters. Did we stop her? Will she come back?"

The sound of his weak voice, cracked with desperation, broke my heart. I didn't know Devecheaux well, but I knew he usually had a deep, booming voice. He'd made a mistake participating in that séance at Seven Sisters, but he'd tried to make amends, hadn't he? He had sent the music box back to us. Buffeted by Isla's angry spirit, he'd fought against her to come to us, to warn us, to help us. That's what I wanted to believe. I hoped it was true. People were still good, right? Some of them, anyway. *Oh Mia, why did things turn out like this?*

I smiled down at him. "No, Isla won't come back. Her power is broken, Henri. She has no more hold on us. We found her secret and exposed it. Tomorrow, the rest of her secrets will be exposed too. People will know what she did, who she really was. Louis Beaumont will be given a proper burial. It's all okay."

"Thank the Lord. Oh goodness, I can't believe this happened to me. I've never had to battle anything like that."

Ashland said, "Mr. Devecheaux, I'm going to have to ask you to please keep this off your website. CJ told me that you have some kind of supernatural website featuring old houses in Mobile, but I don't want what happened tonight to show up there. Please. Getting rid of Isla was a step in the right direction, but I have a feeling that's not the end of the story. Somehow I know we haven't met the most dangerous thing yet." He paused and looked at me, his eyes wide at his own confession. This was all new territory for him. "I've got to find a missing girl, and sharing this all over the Internet won't help me. If you agree to keep quiet, I'll reward you for your trouble."

I just looked at Ashland. Even though I knew he was concerned for Seven Sisters, I was surprised he was even raising this issue. But I kept my mouth shut and just listened to the conversation.

The big man smiled. "That's mighty kind of you two. I appreciate that, and you can count on me. I won't tell a soul. Not even Mia, if she ever came around again."

"Thanks, Henri. Why don't you get some sleep...we'll come see you in the morning."

"That will be fine, but I have to tell you what I saw." He reached for my hand with his own cold, clammy one. He rubbed the back of my hand and closed his eyes for a minute.

"It was Isla that led you to the Moonlight Garden, wasn't it, Henri?"

"She did, CJ, but that's not everything. I saw a man there too, a handsome man with angry dark eyes, dark hair, a fancy hat and a white collared shirt. He watched us from the edge and didn't come close. He watched Isla. When he saw she failed, he turned and walked away. Right into the mist..."

"Must have been the captain. Captain David Garrett. What else did you see?"

"I saw the young lady, Cal...Cal..."

"Calpurnia?"

"Yes, she was standing beside Ashland in the garden. She was smiling and clapping when he opened the bag, and then she disappeared."

I smiled at Ashland too. The old Ashland would have stormed out of the room and run away from all this, but this was not the old Ashland. He had a new respect for the supernatural, I imagined. I suspected he had some abilities too, although he probably wasn't ready to talk about them yet.

"Thanks for telling us." I squeezed Devecheaux's oversized hand, ready to leave him to rest. He was going to need it.

"Now wait! I saw someone with you too."

I froze. Who would be following me? My father? I'd never seen him or met him, and I didn't know if he was dead or alive. I didn't even know who he was. Did Devecheaux mean my mother was dead? We never talked, and I was fairly sure she didn't love me, couldn't love me...mental illness was so cruel. But I had always imagined I would know if she were dead.

"I saw a young man, about as tall as you." Devecheaux smiled like he knew a secret. An amazing, happy secret. "A fine figure who wore black trousers, a black vest and a billowing white shirt. He had dark skin, very dark skin, and short dark hair. That boy had intelligent eyes and full lips. I didn't catch his name—I think he is known by a few, if that makes sense."

"It's Muncie." Tears filled my eyes. I supposed he was there to be close to Calpurnia. He was her closest friend, and she was his. "Was he with Callie?"

"No, he was with you, always staying close to you."

I blinked tears out of my eyes, not understanding what he was saying. "That's got to be a mistake. He was Calpurnia's dearest friend. He must have been there to watch what was happening or at the very least protect her from Isla."

Devecheaux's face fell. "I know what I saw. That boy was there protecting you, just like Calpurnia was watching over Mr. Stuart. When you hunkered down beside me, he was there too. He had kind eyes, full of love and sympathy." He contemplated me for a moment and said, "There's nothing to be ashamed of."

I turned beet red and said, "I'm not ashamed of Muncie; I just don't understand. I just assumed...I mean...Callie is related to Ashland, but could I be related to Muncie? I don't know much about my own bloodline, so it's possible, I suppose." I couldn't understand what he meant, but the man was sick. Maybe he just needed to rest. I squeezed his hand. "We can talk about this tomorrow. Now get some rest."

Ashland and I lingered by the door, whispering to one another. It appeared that Devecheaux had finally fallen asleep. I was glad. Suddenly, I had an idea. "I need to sleep with those jewels."

"What?" he said with a laugh.

"Seriously, I need to sleep with them to see who I dream about; it might help us find Calpurnia. Look, I'm not going to steal them."

"I didn't say you would." Ashland shook his head, rolling his eyes.

"Well, we need to find Calpurnia, right?"

"How do you know that will work? You said so yourself—that's not a sure method. What if you end up dreaming about another murderer or something? Carrie Jo, you have no idea what doors you'll be opening, and I can't go with you. I hate to think of you fighting with the ghost of Jeremiah Cottonwood alone!"

"Well, I'll amp up the power, then. I plan on dreaming in the house."

"No way!" he nearly shouted. "That's not going to happen. You can't sleep on the property; you'll dream the whole time. Something significant is always happening there."

"Come on, Ashland. You want me to find Calpurnia just as much as I do. This is the way to do it."

"This is the wrong way. No cheating. I want you to find her the regular way, like a historian. And you're an excellent historian. Promise me?"

"I know this will work if I do it correctly. I'm getting better at it."

"No!" It was Devecheaux's rough voice pleading with us from his hospital bed. "Please don't do whatever you're planning, CJ. You should know—Isla isn't the only ghost in that house. There are other things left undone, other secrets that you don't know about. Sometimes it's better to leave some things in the dark. Promise me?"

I could hear his heart monitor beeping fast, then faster and faster. I felt compelled to agree. "Okay, okay, I won't. For now. Goodnight, Henri. See you in the morning."

"I'll see you then. I promise you, I'll be right as rain."

Chapter Seven

By nine o'clock the next day, an archaeological dig began right behind the mausoleum at Seven Sisters. It wasn't a coincidence, but we had to give Louis Beaumont a proper burial, hopefully with as little police involvement as possible. The less the police department knew, the better. It was easy enough to tell Detective Simmons some family legends about a lost uncle who died on the property sometime between 1830 and 1850. The coroner came out to take a look at the bones and agreed with Professor Wachowski of the University of South Alabama; the remains were of a man who died from blunt force trauma to the head almost two hundred years ago. The plan was to allow USA to do a full examination of the bones, and then we would place Beaumont inside the mausoleum next to his beloved sister. Things moved smoothly, almost too smoothly to be believed.

I stopped by the hospital before I went to Seven Sisters, but to my surprise Henri Devecheaux wasn't there. According to the nurse, he checked himself out without leaving a note, a phone number or anything. I felt a deep sense of loss—I barely knew him, but I liked him. I think he'd been caught up in the whirlwind, an unexpected near-casualty of the machinations of a malevolent ghost. I hoped he would be safe, no matter where he went.

The weeks went by, and I was soon distracted with a dozen tasks. I began to notice that the house had quieted somehow. The frenetic excitement that had vibrated right underneath the surface during our initial months of restoration had vanished. The house felt empty, but somewhere in the wings, something waited—some pending experience that hadn't manifested yet. Or maybe it had happened but was doomed to repeat itself. I shivered. *Doomed.* Why would that word come to mind?

I watched TD walk from room to room with his clipboard, writing furiously on his many checklists. I didn't bother attempting to engage him in conversation. He barely spoke to me anymore, or to Ashland. He had made it clear that he wanted this job to be over and never wanted to come back here again. Privately, I had talked to Ashland about letting TD go because he couldn't handle what he'd witnessed. But Ashland had refused, even though TD wouldn't talk to him beyond a "yes" or "no." I thought the three of us had been not just colleagues but friends. Now the closeness we'd developed during the restoration had vanished—another unfortunate casualty of the supernatural activity that seemed to ooze from the house.

He was aloof with Ashland and me, but he'd gotten quite close to Detra Ann. She stopped by frequently to bring him lunch or a coffee in the morning. As the old southern belles would say, "she'd set her cap for him." He didn't mind, apparently; just a few days after the lunch deliveries, I spotted him kissing her in his truck. *Good for you, Terrence Dale! Back to the land of the living, I see.* I waved at them as I walked to my car at the end of the day without waiting to see if they waved back. I didn't want to know.

On the other hand, my whirlwind romance with Ashland had come to a screeching halt. He'd developed a new habit—daydreaming. It interrupted everything: staff meetings, one-on-one conversations, even his interactions with vendors and subcontractors. I had no idea what was going on in his head, and it didn't seem like he wanted to share it with me. That stung, but I had some processing to do too. At least Calpurnia's treasure had been recovered; all the pieces now were in the safekeeping of a trusted local jeweler who would attempt to appraise each item. I'm sure his findings would be staggering—even for Ashland, who was no stranger to wealth. Somehow, Ashland had managed to keep the news of the discovery under wraps, but I knew that wouldn't last long. People always talked, didn't they?

The month had slipped by, and now we were in the dog days of August. I looked forward to September when we might get a reprieve from the unbearable heat. I'd spent one Friday afternoon working in the glass case in the upstairs hallway. I was so proud of the unique collection of hand-painted fans we were displaying. They had come from local families anxious to be a part of the Seven Sisters story. Even after all these years, the house was still a landmark, an enduring part of local culture. I closed the case with a sigh of pleasure.

When I left Seven Sisters that day, my goal had been to quietly slip out with another treasure I had squirreled away in my purse. Rachel K. and I had dug through the last remaining trunk, an extremely old one with a cracked leather lid, and it was there that I found the treasure hidden. It was an old schoolroom book with brittle paper and faded ink. The inner pages displayed beautiful penmanship and some painfully long sentences. Nothing like what you would see students using today. I didn't know whose book it was until I started scanning through it. And then there it was: "My name is Monticello..." I held my breath as I read the next few paragraphs. Some pages were poems that he'd copied, probably at the behest of a teacher like Christine or Calpurnia. This was no journal—not intimate details about his life—but it was proof that he'd been here. Now I had something I could dream with! More than ever, the idea of hiding out in my comfortable apartment for a session of dream catching appealed to me. I'd fallen out of the habit in the past few weeks and for some reason hadn't cracked open any of Calpurnia's journals. It was like a quiet voice inside my head said, "No, not yet."

Bette was going on a long weekend trip with her beau. She was so excited about the excursion, and I couldn't help but grin thinking about her bouncing curls and big smile. That meant it would be Bienville and me, but if I decided to slip away, there was always something to do in Mobile—a music festival or some kind of food fest happening. I absently thought of William. I supposed he'd gone back home by now or moved on with his tour. Despite how things had turned out, I believed William had liked me in his own way. But Mia had fallen for him hard...unbeknownst to me, of course. I shook my head and slung my purse strap over my shoulder. *Think of something else!*

I hoped Ashland and I could connect again somehow. My feelings for him hadn't changed, but I was a bit more cautious now. No matter—at least not this weekend. I intended to focus my energy on learning more about Muncie. I thought of the young man, his vibrant brown eyes and soft voice. I wondered if perhaps we were connected somehow, by spirit if not by blood. It was a nice thought.

I knew things about him. I knew Muncie's secret: he could read brilliantly, write well and work basic math equations, thanks to Christine Cottonwood and her daughter. I remembered that he felt very smart for knowing all these things. Above everything else, though, he had one burning desire—he wanted to go home.

Home for him was not the faraway land of Africa, like it was for so many slaves who arrived in Mobile. His home had been Port-au-Prince, Haiti. An uncle had waited until his mother had left the house, lied to the slavers and claimed that the little boy had been his slave. Too small to explain himself to the English-speaking slavers, Muncie had been stolen from his mother, who would cry for him every day, beating her breast with her fist and praying for her boy's return.

I couldn't explain how I knew all this. Perhaps from the dreams, or maybe I had read it in Calpurnia's journals, but I knew it. I reached into my purse and touched the fabric-covered book, feeling comforted. This book could be the key to so many secrets. I didn't need to sleep at Seven Sisters; I might be able to see what I needed without putting myself in danger.

"Hey, Carrie Jo! Do you have a minute?"

Rachel sounded like she had something on her mind. It seemed I wasn't going to get away so easily. "What is it, Rachel?"

"I've heard...I mean, Detra Ann told us that something happened here the night of the Moonlight Garden tour. That a ghost showed up afterward. That can't be true, right?"

I couldn't tell if she wanted it to be true or not, but I knew I had to be practical—and as honest as I could be. "Have you ever seen a ghost here?"

"Well, no, but there are times I feel creeped out. Like someone is watching me or something. I even thought I heard someone giggling once, but there was no one there. I've never actually seen anything, though."

"Well, it is a very old house. Which is why we are all here, of course!" I chuckled, and then gave her a comforting smile. "I did see something that night, but it's gone now, and I don't think it will bother anyone again. You don't have to be afraid."

She gave an audible sigh of relief. "Oh, good, because I don't think I could handle that."

"If you ever do see something, feel free to talk to me, Rachel." I smiled and waved goodbye to her as I got into the car.

Well, talk was bound to happen. Detra Ann was full of information, wasn't she?

I decided not to worry about it. I couldn't stop people from talking. Right as I swung into my empty driveway, my phone rang. It was Ashland. "Hey, what's up?"

"Does something need to be up?" He chuckled softly, sounding happier and more relaxed than he had in a long time. "What are you doing this evening?"

"What time?" I felt conflicted. I had Muncie's book to go through, but it was hard to say no to Ashland when he was ready to spend some time with me.

"Around sunset?"

I looked at my watch. It was five, but the sun didn't go down until sometime around seven in the middle of the summer. "I don't know. I planned on sitting in front of the television with a bag of Doritos. Why, you want to join me?"

"That doesn't sound like you at all—I have a better idea. Let me pick you up, and we'll take a walk along the beach on

Dauphin Island. Afterward, maybe we'll go to Barnacle Bill's for a quiet dinner. What do you say?"

I smiled as I turned the car off. "I say yes. That sounds nice, Ashland. What time will you pick me up?"

"In about thirty minutes? It will take us another half-hour to get to the island, but I think you'll love it."

"Great! Sounds perfect."

"All right, see you in thirty."

My heart fluttered with anticipation. I hurriedly went through my scanty closet looking for appropriate clothing. Fortunately, I'd recently purchased some nice clothes at University Mall, but I wished I had taken the time to do laundry that week. *Oh well.* I reached for a pretty lilac handkerchief skirt and a cream-colored peasant blouse, and then I haphazardly ripped off the tags. I had some strappy tan sandals that would work well with this ensemble. *Perfect for strolling down a beach with Ashland.*

I heard scratching at the door and found fat Bienville looking forlorn and hungry. "Come on, chubby. You're on your own tonight, though. I have a date!" Then I spotted Iberville at the edge of the porch. The white cat was perched on the railing, his tail flicking. I called to him, hoping to pet him as a thank you for saving me from Mia, but he chose to ignore me again. That was okay. I could love him from a distance—I'd seen those claws in action. I put some water in a dish for Bienville and headed to the bathroom to get ready. My phone rang again, and I picked it up laughing, thinking it was Ashland. It wasn't. I heard Alice Reed's voice on the phone.

"Carrie Jo? Is that you? This is Alice."

"Hello, Mrs. Reed. Yes, this is Carrie Jo." I sat on the side of the bed, holding my breath. What would I say? *Just tell the truth, CJ.*

"I'm sorry to call like this, but we need your help." I could imagine Alice's stiff bouffant hairstyle shaking as she spoke. She and Myron were good people, always kind to everyone. "We are in Mobile, at the Battle House. We have talked with Mia. Carrie Jo, she is willing to turn herself in, but she wants to talk to you first. I know it won't matter much, and I know she's done wrong. But she's pretty insistent, and I'd like to talk to you too." Her voice lowered, and she spoke in a careful, respectful way. "My daughter isn't well, Carrie Jo. She hasn't been for a long time..."

She seemed well enough when she attacked me, I thought, but I didn't say that. I respected Alice too much. "Is she sick?"

"No. Well, yes, but not physically. It's another kind of sickness."

"Oh." I had firsthand knowledge of the other kind of sickness. My mother had battled mental illness all her life. How had I handled it? By avoiding her, giving up on her. Running away as often as I could. Mental illness was a cruel disease, but there were times I was sad and ashamed about the way I had handled things. Had I really done all I could for Momma?

"There's more to it than that. Anyway, may we please meet with you in the morning? Just me and Myron and then Mia? I feel like we owe you an explanation."

"You don't owe me anything, Mrs. Reed. You were always good to me, but Mia has tried to hurt me, twice. I hope she does get help. Believe it or not, I care about her."

"We know you do. When she comes back to herself, she will remember that too. May we meet with you in the morning? Here at our hotel? Say about 8 a.m.?"

"Sure, I'll be there. Actually, 9 works better if that's okay with you. What room?"

"Yes, we can do 9. We will meet you in the lobby—we can talk there. Thank you, Carrie Jo."

I hung up the phone, feeling relieved that they'd found Mia, spoken to her. I hoped she would turn herself in. Perhaps since Isla's "spell" was broken, it was broken over Mia too. I could only hope. Maybe things were going to be okay with her after all. I stroked Bienville's orange fur and then went to take a quick shower. I needed to rinse away the sweat. No matter how cool it was in the house, just stepping outdoors for a second made me feel like a wilted flower. I wouldn't have time to wash my hair, so I pulled it up into a ponytail on top of my head and put on a shower cap.

For the first time in a long time, I sang in the shower. It felt good to tap into my inner diva, but I was thankful no one could hear me except Bienville, who hopped up on the counter to listen to the free concert.

He didn't stay long. I didn't take it personally.

Chapter Eight

Always on time, Ashland didn't disappoint. He arrived just when he said he would. But I didn't run out of the house like a teenager when he pulled up. I let him come upstairs first. I'd learned a thing or two from Calpurnia—ladies didn't run down the stairs and jump in cars or carriages. I was glad that Ashland had the manners of a true southern gentleman. I peeped at him as he walked up the stairs. I loved the color of his hair and how soft it looked. Make no mistake, though. Ashland wasn't anything but manly. I recognized his blue linen shirt, and my mind wandered back to that hot, sticky day when we walked to the mausoleum. The color matched his eyes, and I loved that shade on him. He wore casual khakis and a copper and leather bracelet. I was glad we were on the same wavelength as far as the dress code. *I think I got this outfit right.*

After he knocked politely, I opened the door, welcoming him with a smile. "You look great," he said, smiling appreciatively. "But then, you always do."

"Thanks, Ashland. Come on, Bienville. You can't stay in here by yourself. I don't know what you'll get into." The orange tabby flopped down beside me in a sign of protest. "No, I'm sorry. Those are the rules. No kitty home alone here." I scooped him up and carried him outside. Ashland locked the apartment for me, and I set Bienville free to play with his brother.

Ashland took my hand and led me down the wooden stairs into the warm afternoon. His hand felt warm and comforting. I hadn't realized how much I liked holding hands until I met him. We exchanged a few small smiles as we made our way to his car. He opened the car door for me, and I hopped in as elegantly as I could. Ashland took the wheel, and soon we were driving to the southernmost part of Mobile County.

He grinned at me. "Well, history lover, you will find the island fascinating. I know I do. The rumors are that DeSoto explored the area sometime around 1540, but it was the French that officially claimed the island in 1699. It's much smaller than it was once—it is a barrier island, but there's still some of the original topography left. A half dozen hurricanes have changed the island's shape several times, and pirates even razed it in the 1700s, but it's still a beautiful place. Serene, with sandy white beaches."

"Sounds like my kind of place. Do you come down here often?"

"Honestly, not as much as I used to. My mother and I used to stay at an East End beach house every year for a month or so. We'd come down, dig around for shells, visit the mounds, snack on shrimp. Those were nice summers. I didn't come back after she passed, not right away anyway. When I was a teen, I spent most of my beach time at Gulf Shores. That's where all the action is—lots of clubs and restaurants and girls in bikinis." He grinned at me, blushing slightly. "Dauphin Island is much more laid back than the panhandle beaches. No big buildings except for a condo or two, and definitely no teen clubs."

"Sounds like heaven. I was never one to frequent teen clubs." I laughed at the idea. My ultra-religious mother would have never gone for that. "Thanks for giving me the island tour. Dauphin Island sounds like an intriguing place to visit. I admit that I haven't been a very good tourist, but I love Mobile. It's a friendly place. Good vibes here. Mostly," I added quickly.

"That's good to hear. I was afraid that you'd be ready to leave as soon as you could." The concern in his voice sounded genuine. I hated to hear that he had doubts about my fortitude; honestly, I hadn't even thought about leaving Mobile or Seven Sisters. But then again, I wasn't your average girl.

"I have no plans to leave, Ashland. I'm still committed to finding Calpurnia. Aren't you?"

His handsome face relaxed a bit, and he gave me a wistful smile as we crossed the bridge that would take us to the island. "More than ever. I'm happy to hear that. I was hoping Terrence Dale would change his mind and stick around, but I'm afraid he's not going to. He won't say it, but I know it's about our garden visitor. I don't blame him, but he's the best contractor in Mobile—actually, the best contractor on the entire Gulf Coast as far as I'm concerned, and they aren't in short supply around here. Losing TD is going to put us behind on the opening at the very least."

"Maybe we could talk to him, together. Try to explain what happened. Well, not explain it...I mean, who could explain that? But maybe start a conversation about it." I gave him a nervous smile. It couldn't hurt, could it? It hadn't seemed right to force TD to talk to me, but now I guessed we had to. Ashland had every reason to be concerned, and we couldn't lose him if we could avoid it. He knew so much about the house and preservation, and besides, I liked him.

"Let's do that. I think with any luck, Detra Ann will help us." Ashland turned right on Bienville Boulevard, the island's main road, and I couldn't help but stare at my surroundings.

Dauphin Island had lots of pines and a few hearty palm trees. I'd been to Pensacola Beach once; it was nothing like this place. Despite the scattered beach houses and the massive water tank that greeted us as we drove onto the island, it had a sense of wildness. Yes, lots of history had happened here. I could feel that. What had those first settlers thought when they walked the beaches for the first time? We drove past a few seafood shops, more beach houses and a few duplexes. I spotted the wooden sign that announced the public beach. We drove down Bienville Boulevard to the West End.

"The public beach isn't as nice as the West End Beach. Won't take but a few minutes to get there—just in time for the sunset." Ashland smiled at me, his hair catching the fading sunshine like a golden halo. "You'll notice that there's no cell signal out here on this end of the island. Not much of anything except a long stretch of beach."

"So I'm going to be sitting on a beach watching the sunset with a handsome man and with no cell phones to interrupt us? Sounds perfect." I wasn't too good at flirting, but I must have done it right. It gave me butterflies to see him blush. A few minutes later, we pulled into a small parking lot; there were only two other cars there, but there was plenty of evidence the beach had been busy earlier. An abandoned floatie lay in the sand, tire tracks were everywhere and a lone lifeguard was closing his shack for the day. "You folks stay out of the water. Rip current this afternoon," the young man called to us.

"No problem. We don't plan on swimming," Ashland called back to him, giving him a friendly wave. He walked to his trunk, popped it open and took out a comfy-looking blanket, presumably for us to sit on as we enjoyed the scenery. Sunset was only minutes away now. We wore shades, but I had fun imagining his sexy blue eyes behind those stylish frames.

I slid off my shoes and enjoyed the warmth of the sand under my feet. It must have been a scorcher in the afternoon, but the evening ocean breeze cooled everything down. Happy with the spot he found, Ashland awkwardly spread out the blanket. I helped, and soon we settled down to enjoy nature's display.

"I'm surprised you didn't want to take the Happy Go Lucky out. I bet sunsets from the boat are real showstoppers."

"Yes, they are, but we wouldn't have had time today. I hope this is okay?"

I slid my arm through his and inched a little closer. "This is perfect."

Ashland leaned in, his lips almost touching mine. I closed my eyes behind my sunglasses, preparing for a kiss that didn't come. Then I opened them again and found him looking at me with a confident smile. He'd removed his sunglasses and was sliding mine up to the top of my head.

"I want to see your lovely green eyes. I love those eyes, Carrie Jo. May I kiss you now?" I nodded, and our lips met softly. His hand cupped my chin, and his thumb rubbed my jaw. I leaned even closer and curled my arms around his waist. He held me after I pulled away gently, and we stayed like that for a few seconds before he whispered, "Look at that." I turned to see the orange sun low on the horizon, seeming to dip into the ocean. The dimming orb left traces of red and gold in the sky. A few clouds lingered on the horizon, black and purple against the fading brightness.

"Wow, that's amazing. Thank you for this. I needed this moment." I squeezed his hand, wanting to kiss him again. I liked kissing him, that was for sure, but I had to keep it together. *Too late for that, CJ. You've already kissed him a half dozen times. Why stop now?* It had been so long since I'd been intimate with someone, and I found the temptation to succumb to my own needs difficult to resist. And the longer we sat there, the harder it was. Even if his intentions were as pure as the driven snow, mine weren't. I'd always prided myself on being a "head over heart" kind of girl, but what I felt for Ashland was unlike anything I'd felt before. I couldn't explain it.

Slowly, we leaned back on the blanket, his arms around me. I could hear the waves crashing nearby, but my thoughts were completely on the man beside me. I never dreamed I'd be lying on a blanket at the beach with Ashland. Who was in control of my life?

My hands ran instinctively up and down his arms...I loved the feeling of his muscular body. We kissed more deeply, and my hands curled in his hair. When I heard him murmur my name in my ear, the electricity was palpable. *Oh my God, I can't do this!* I pushed away gently—I had to catch my breath. His blue eyes were intense and full of passion. I felt the same way, but we couldn't do this here, not now. I leaned back on the blanket and closed my eyes. I felt Ashland lie down beside me. If we lingered on the beach much longer the sky would be full of stars.

"I'm sorry, I didn't mean to get carried away."

"Stop apologizing for everything. You didn't force me to kiss you." I punched his arm playfully and sat up, looking down at him.

He reached up and touched my hair, twisting a long strand around his finger. "You make me crazy, Carrie Jo. What am I going to do about you?"

"I guess you'll just have to love me." *Oh my God, I just said love. Get me out of here.* I stood up and pretended to dust sand off, avoiding looking at his face. "Why don't we take a little walk? I could use the exercise. Let me help you with that blanket." He seemed surprised but got the hint; I helped him fold it, and we strolled down the beach toward the very tip of the island.

"So how are *you* doing? We talked about TD, but what about you? We haven't talked much since that night in the garden." A sensible change of topic was in order.

He stuffed the blanket under his arm and slung his hands in his pockets as we walked. "Carrie Jo, you know I have never been a fan of the supernatural, but what happened with us in the garden made me a believer. I guess I haven't wanted to talk about it because I didn't know what to say. I saw Isla with my own two eyes, felt the wind ripping through the trees. We even found the family treasure, but admitting the reality of it all has been extremely difficult. That might make me sound stupid, but it's the truth." As we walked on a little more, I breathed in the ocean scent and savored being here with Ashland. "It didn't seem to faze you at all. I mean you acted like you knew exactly what was happening and how to handle it. How do you live with your...well, for lack of a better word, your powers?"

"Are you kidding me?" I gave him a wide-eyed stare. "That was the scariest thing that ever happened to me. Everything I did—I played all that by ear. I have no experience with ghosts at all. Except in my dreams, and normally they don't try to hurt me." *Except that time Jeremiah Cottonwood left a welt on my leg.* "Not to mention, I think we had help. Remember, Henri said that Calpurnia and Muncie were there too."

"And you believe him?"

"Why wouldn't I? Henri has nothing to lose or gain by telling us what he saw." I chewed on the inside of my lip. "I hope he's okay. I mean, I pray that she left him alone."

"Me too."

"You didn't answer my question, Ashland. Are you okay?" We had walked a long stretch down the beach, and the sand felt a bit cooler. He took my hand and we began to walk back to the car.

"I have to be. I'm Ashland Stuart, former football star and heir to the Stuart fortune, which is substantially more now than it was six months ago, thanks to you." He grimaced. "Am I okay? I'm sleeping again now and not jumping at every noise I hear, but something else has happened to me."

I froze in my tracks, curious to hear more. "What is happening?"

"I am remembering things, things from my childhood. Things I don't want to remember. I sound like a basket case, huh?"

"Hardly a basket case, Ashland. You have a long way to go before I check you in somewhere. Oh, sorry." The look on his face reminded me that this kind of talk was no laughing matter. In some ways, Ashland and I were more alike than I had first believed, at least concerning our families. "What do you mean, remembering?"

"I've been accused of having an active imagination, at least when I was a kid. Mostly by my cousin Robert, who passed on his loathing for the supernatural to me, but it wasn't always like that. I swear, and this is the crazy part, I remember that I saw Calpurnia. I'd forgotten all about her, but I did see her once. It was during those days in the garden, the Rose Garden. I always hated going into the Moonlight Garden, and now I know why, but it was different in the Rose Garden."

"Did she say anything to you? You weren't afraid, were you?"

"No, she didn't say anything. To be honest, she didn't seem to notice me at first."

"Really?" I put my hand on his arm. "What happened?"

"Mother was trying to prune some of the rose bushes, and I was sitting on the grass by a concrete bench reading a book. I didn't notice the visitor at first, but I kind of felt the air shift and knew someone else was there. I looked up, and standing a few feet away was a young woman, very slender and tall, with an elegant hairstyle on top of her head. She knelt down beside me to peek at what I was reading. I know now that was Calpurnia. I mean, I've seen her picture before in the brochures, but I never put two and two together. At least not until recently. I clearly remember that she smiled at me, and I wasn't afraid at all so I smiled back. She showed me her book: it was small, a little larger than her hand, and it had a leather cover. When she opened it to show me what was inside, it wasn't a regular book, just a bunch of folded notes tied together with a purple ribbon. I guess she wanted me to see that she was reading too."

We started walking again. I whispered, "I've seen that book before, I think. Did it have an engraving on the cover—a bird sitting on a branch?"

He thought for a minute. "Yes, I believe it did, right in the center of the cover. Do you know what book it was?"

"Yes, oh my gosh. I think I do!" He put the blanket in the trunk, and we got into the car. I could feel him watching me in the near dark. "That's the book she kept the notes in, the ones from the captain."

"I don't understand. Why would she keep Captain Garrett's notes in a book? I've never heard of that."

"I saw her father search her room once, but I got the feeling that he'd done it before. He looked through everything: her clothing, her hatboxes, everything you could think of to find Christine's treasure. What would he have done if he'd found those notes? It wasn't a clue to the treasure, but it would have put her in a dangerous position, especially with Mr. Cottonwood's pride. She was a clever girl. Hiding them in plain sight, in a hollowed-out book, would be the smart thing to do. The question is why did she show you the book? What was she trying to say?"

"I don't know, CJ. So I'm not losing it?"

"No, you saw her all right. You don't have any reason to be afraid of her. She'd never harm you, but I think she wants you to know something." A shiver ran down my spine.

"It's getting cool out here. Let's go eat at Bill's. They close up the sidewalks here around nine, so we better go if we want a seat. No more talk of ghosts tonight. Let's talk about living."

I was disappointed not to hear more but happy that he'd confided in me at last. It had been quite an evening already.

"Find us something good on the radio," he said with a soft smile.

"I can do that." I flipped the channels in search of a good song, and we talked about practical things like his upcoming speech at the Historical Society and the custom-made, very expensive velvet curtains for the Blue Room.

In the back of my mind, I knew what I had to do. This was going to be a late night.

Chapter 9

Strange music, a kind I'd never heard before, plunked from a piano on the boat. I knew it was a piano because Mrs. Cottonwood often played the big shiny black one in the ballroom, but this music was different. No long strands of silver notes here or heart-aching songs of love, but plunking notes that piled up together and made your feet want to move.

I never touched the big black piano, but I had wanted to. What if there were silver notes in my fingertips too? Shouldn't I let them have their song? Mrs. Cottonwood would probably never have scolded me—that gentle lady would never harm a fly—but Stokes would have beaten me with a hickory stick. I got smacked once for looking too long in a mirror. I missed the lady—she'd been nice with soft hands and a softer voice, but her death had not surprised me. Mr. Cottonwood was a cruel man, especially when he had turned up a jug a few times, but no one had suffered more from his words and hands than Mrs. Cottonwood.

How many times had I wanted to grab his arm or take a lash for her? But fear kept me from doing so, my completely miserable and undeniable fear. Hooney had warned me to stay out of the reach of the Master's strap. Once he started swinging he wouldn't stop, not until he passed out. She should know—she'd been at Seven Sisters for ages, longer than anyone except Stokes, but she'd only been beaten once. One stormy evening when we huddled around the kitchen fire for warmth, Hooney told me the story of Ann-Sheila, a pretty slave who had belonged to the Beaumont family before Mrs. Cottonwood came to Seven Sisters.

Like me, Ann-Sheila was an island slave, a free woman before someone snatched her away from her home. Hooney said she was *the most beautiful girl she'd ever seen, and she was smart too—way too smart for a slave. Ann-Sheila loved Mrs. Cottonwood, not like a slave but like a sister or a good friend. Stokes and Hooney said that was wrong, wrong to think a slave could be the friend of a free person, especially a white person. Ann-Sheila could read, like me, and sometimes the Missus would ask her to read aloud from one of the many books in the library.*

One evening, after Mr. Cottonwood had been in town for a few days of gambling, he came racing his horse down the lane, his anger stirred up from corn whiskey. They say he must have heard some bit of gossip in town, something about the Missus or Ann-Sheila or maybe both. He was powerful offended by gossip and had a great deal of pride for his family name. I don't know what the gossip was, but Mr. Cottonwood went looking for Miss Christine with murder on his mind. He found her in the nursery with Ann-Sheila and the baby Calpurnia, and in his rage had struck his wife and daughter. Ann-Sheila slapped the belt from his hands, but she should never have done that. No, she should never have done that.

The Master took Ann-Sheila to the slave quarters and made all the folks come out to see what he was going to do to his wife's pretty young friend. He'd summoned the sheriff, the nasty one with the greasy black mustache, to deliver the punishment. The Master shamed Ann-Sheila by taking her clothes off and forcing her down on one of the big wooden tables in the middle of the quarter. He didn't actually do the bad deed—the sheriff did that—but the whole time the sheriff was doing what he wanted, Ann-Sheila cursed him and Mr. Cottonwood until Mr. Cottonwood ordered Stokes to put his hand over her mouth to stop the curses. After the sheriff did what he wanted to do, Mr.

Cottonwood made some of the slaves do the same thing. Some was old men and some was just boys. Everyone did what they was told, and even today nobody talks about what they did to Ann-Sheila. They turn and look the other way when passing the table, making the sign of the cross if her name is uttered, but nobody much utters her name in the quarter. You won't find nary a slave at Seven Sisters sitting at that table either.

When the deed was done, they say she crawled off the wooden table and started screaming and talking to people that weren't there. People say she cursed the Master in her island language, and other people say she cursed everyone that did the bad things to her. Hooney said she had blood all over her because the Master whipped her to the ground after the deed was done. It was all too horrible to think of. Ann-Sheila walked down to the river, and nobody stopped her. The Master laughed and laughed with his belt in his hand, mocking her, calling her names and such. When she got to the water, she threw her bloody self in with not a stitch of clothes on and floated away. Sometime later, some slaves pulled her out, and Hooney said that there was nobody ever been more dead than Ann-Sheila. The Master had her body put on a pile of wood, and he burned her up. "First that long dark hair caught fire, then the rest of her," Hooney whispered, her large eyes looking even more huge and luminous. "And the Master made the Missus watch too. Poor lady. She couldn't speak for days after that, but eventually she came round again. Horrible, horrible day. A cursed day." She'd finished her recounting with the sign of the cross and a few other signs that I didn't recognize.

Now here I was doing the same thing as Ann-Sheila, helping someone escape the wrath of Mr. Cottonwood. And not just anyone but the Master's own daughter! I stood on the bank of that river, trembling in my uncomfortable shoes and talking to God, telling Him why I wanted to live another day, but I was sure I wouldn't. I had nowhere to go except into the river. Tears streamed down my face like two fountains of salt water. Hooney's warning rang in my ear: "You knows too much—too much for a slave. You thinks too deep to live too long. You a dead man, Muncie, if you don't stop thinking. You a dead man." She'd prayed, sometimes for me and sometimes against me, twisting the worn edge of her white apron. I wanted to yell at her, "That is not my name! I am no dead man!" but I never did.

I hunkered down in the scratchy reeds and stared at the big boat. I would wait right here until I knew she was gone, safely away. Then I would run to the Mobile Bay Port, not the river port but the big one with the big ships. I would find a way to steal aboard a ship, and maybe that ship would take me home and once again I would be who I really was—I could have my name again.

I guessed if the dogs came for me, those snarling hounds of Jeremiah Cottonwood's, I'd do like Ann-Sheila—I would jump in the river even though it wasn't a smart thing to jump in the Mobile River at night. There was snakes in that river—cottonmouths that could kill a man with one bite. If the snakes didn't kill me, perhaps the alligators would. Me and Early saw one snap a raccoon right off the shore one day. We were little then and weren't serving in the house yet. The two of us snuck off to splash and swim, and when we were finally tuckered out we sat on the bank to catch our breath before heading back to the quarter. All of a sudden that gator raged up and out of the water, snapping that coon, and then slid back into the black depths. Early had screamed, but I'd taken off running.

I thought about my choices, snake bites, alligator bites or dog bites. Those dogs were nothing but mean. I remember once they'd gotten into the rabbits—Calpurnia's pet rabbits—and left nothing behind but torn bits of fluff all over the ground like a furry hailstorm of death and guts and blood. I had to clean it all up and gagged the whole time. But even with all the dangers around me, I couldn't leave. Not without knowing for sure that she was gone, safely away from the hands of death that reached for her from Seven Sisters. I didn't want her to die like Miss Christine or disappear like Louis Beaumont. She must live because I loved her.

I stood in the tall reeds without moving, like one of those statues at Seven Sisters, frozen in time forever. I heard a limb snap and looked about me, half-expecting to see Isla standing in my hiding spot. It was unearthly how she moved about without anyone hearing her—like a Haitian demon, one that played tricks on naughty, unsuspecting children. Some demons could come up through the floor of a house, grab you from a tree or get you any number of ways. My mother told me that you could summon one up just by thinking about it or saying its secret name too many times. I believed whether she was a Haitian demon or a plain old Alabama devil in pretty white skin, Isla lived to torment me.

One morning, I woke up and she was on top of me, straddling me like she was riding a horse. She was light as a feather; I suppose that's why I didn't know she was there until her lips were on mine. She wore nothing but her thin petticoat—too thin for my tastes. My eyes flew open, and I stared into her blue ones. Like two pools of clear blue water they were, but empty, without any life in them. Startled, I pushed her to the ground, and she fell on the floor with a scowl, mustering up a scream at the sound of Stokes' heavy footfall approaching from the hallway. As his dark frame filled the doorway, he threw her a disdainful sneer and stepped out of the way, pointing to the door. "You shouldn't be here, Miss." When she left he struck me to the ground with his oversized hand.

"You stupid boy. Put your shirt on. I told you to stay away from her." I didn't argue with him or try to defend myself—he knew the truth. He was just afraid like we all were.

That same day, Calpurnia had searched me out. Her eyes were red from crying; her hair looked unbrushed and hung free down her back. She'd passed me as I pumped water from the well, giving me the hand signal that meant "Meet me in the greenhouse." I delivered the buckets of water to Hooney, looked over my shoulder a few times to see if the blonde devil dogged my heels and took the long way around to our meeting spot.

Calpurnia's thin arms were around my neck before I had closed the door good. She clung to me like I was the last breath she could take and she wanted to hold on to it. She'd gotten thin—too thin; I could feel her bones beneath the silk of her dress. "Calpurnia, what has happened to you? Are you hungry? You know we can't be here—your cousin, she's always following me. She might tell Stokes or Mr. Cottonwood." Her eyes were green that day; sometimes they looked brown, but that day they were full of heartache. I knew those emotions—fear, hopelessness, grief. They were all I knew for many years, but Calpurnia had helped me. When I cried for my Momma, Calpurnia read to me, sometimes about faraway places with coconut trees and colorful birds—like the ones I left back home.

"I don't want any food. I have to think. I'm sorry for calling you here, but what do I do? What can I do?" She shrugged her

scrawny shoulders at me and handed me a piece of paper. "Look at this—it's a letter from Lennie Ree Meadows. She wants to help me with my wedding because I don't have Momma."

I took the paper and pretended to read it, anxious to see how I could help her but even more anxious to get away. I loved her, but after that morning's encounter with Isla, I had an uneasy feeling that something bad was going to happen. It hung in the air over me like a sword on a string, just like the story of Damocles. Any moment the string would snap, and the sword would come crashing down on me. That would be much worse than getting slapped by Stokes. I heard Hooney's warning ringing in my ears: "You a dead man, Muncie." I loved my friend, but what would happen to us if I was caught in here now?

"What does that mean? Who are you marrying?"

"No one has proposed to me, but Mrs. Meadows seems to think differently. She says my father has made arrangements for me to marry and he didn't bother to tell me. He wants me gone so he can have it all, all my fortune. It's mine because I'm a Beaumont! I know the truth now; Mr. Ball told me, but I can't find it! Mother hid it somewhere, but I don't know where." She rubbed her forehead with her bony hand and kept talking, "I bet half of Mobile thinks I'm going to marry that man. And if they didn't before, they do now! If Mrs. Meadows knows, every gossip in Mobile County knows. What am I going to do? I cannot marry him. I will not!" She snatched away the note and walked up and down the length of the greenhouse talking to herself, her hands on her hips.

"Who is it you're supposed to marry?"

"It's the mayor, that old man, Charles Langdon—the one from Connecticut. He came to my Cotillion Ball, but you

probably wouldn't remember him. He's not a remarkable man except that he's old and likes licking his lips. What shall I do? I'd rather marry Reginald Ball than Charles Langdon, but it's too late. The die is cast."

"Surely she's wrong, Cal. Maybe she's wrong."

She shook the letter at me. "No, she's not wrong, but I'm not going to do it. I won't do it. I'll walk off into the river like Ann-Sheila before I do that." We heard a voice, Isla's voice, calling Calpurnia's name in the distance. It sounded like she was in the Rose Garden. I ducked down, and she squatted with me. "If I go away, please don't worry about me. I will be all right. Promise me you will not worry over me."

"No!" I whispered furiously. "You can't leave. What would your Momma say if you left here with no chaperone and no one to watch over you? I have to go too."

"Don't bring Mother into this. She's gone, and she left me here! I have to go, and I think I know someone who can help me. If I took you with me, it could mean the death of you. I couldn't live with that." She reached out and squeezed my hand. "I love you, Muncie," she said, her voice breaking.

Isla called again, and I could tell she was closer now. So close that I knew she'd find us in just a minute. Calpurnia stuffed the note in her dress pocket. I wanted to argue with her, remind her that I could die either way, whether I was with her or without her, but I didn't have much time. "You can't leave me here. Promise me you'll take me too," I pleaded with her, my heart jumping like a rabbit in my worn cotton shirt.

She sighed but smiled. For a second, I could see her as she used to be, happy, beautiful and full of life. The beautiful storyteller who dreamed of traveling the world with her uncle. "All right, but *we have to be careful. Nobody can know, not even Hooney. Now I have to go. My cousin will find you in here in just a second."*

"Miss...don't trust her. Don't tell her nothing! She's not got a good heart like—she's not good."

"Stop that, Muncie. She's been through so much. You don't understand."

"No, you don't understand, Miss. She's trying to get me into trouble. I can't tell you how many..."

"Shh! Here she comes. I'll go so she won't find you here." She got up and yelled, "I'm in here, Cousin. I'm coming." She walked out of the greenhouse, the rickety wooden door slapping behind her.

I sat on the floor, feeling hopeless. What had I done? What had I agreed to? Mosquitos swirled around me, the angry black insects biting me until I got the courage to slip out of the greenhouse.

If Isla knew anything at all about Calpurnia's plans, it was bad—this would all be bad. Every bit of it.

I woke before the alarm clock and reached over to turn it off. I had an extra thirty minutes to think about what I had dreamed. I closed my eyes and thought of Muncie's strong heart beating in my chest. I remembered the utter desperation on Calpurnia's face. I could see the plants in the greenhouse, smell the fresh earth and hear the buzzing of bees.

I sat up and slid Muncie's workbook out from under the pillow. It had worked, just like I had expected it to. I ran my hand over the cover and flipped my hair back out of my face. I would try it again tonight—I had to know what happened to Calpurnia and Muncie.

A smile crept across my face. That wasn't his name, not his "true born" name. The Master had called him Monticello, and his only friend and her mother had called him Muncie, but these weren't who he was.

He was Janjak.

Chapter 10

I drove down Dauphin Street in my blue Honda to the Battle House Renaissance Mobile Hotel or, as the locals and I preferred to call it, the Battle House. According to local lore, Stephen Douglas spent the night here the very same day he heard he'd lost the election to Abraham Lincoln. It also served as a military headquarters during the War of 1812. I had never stopped to check it out, but it was certainly on my "must do before I leave Mobile" list. Battle House was an eight-story building with Tuscan columns along the portico. I knew some of the history, and under normal circumstances I'd check out every nook and cranny, but not today.

I pulled into the parking lot across the street, slid my phone into my pocket and walked to the hotel. When I pulled open the big glass door, I immediately felt underdressed. Why had I worn blue jeans and a casual shirt to such a beautiful place? I gawked up at the domed stained glass ceiling and the luxurious surroundings. This wasn't where I expected to be, nor was it where I expected to find Alice and Myron. They seemed way too frugal for a swanky place like this, but here we all were. They stood up, spotting me at the same time I saw them, and I took a deep breath and walked toward them. I looked about covertly but didn't see Mia. I slapped a friendly smile on my face and reminded myself that these people had been good to me. It was time to pay them back.

"Carrie Jo, thank you for coming down. We know how busy you must be, and we would never take up your time if we didn't have to."

"It's okay, Alice. I'm glad Mia has agreed to get some help." I hugged her neck and then Myron's. It felt like going home except for Mia's absence.

"Well, Myron? Should you tell this story, or should I?" Alice turned to her husband, who sat quietly on the couch next to her, his grief-filled eyes huge behind thick eyeglasses.

"No, dear, I'll let you do all the talking. As a matter of fact, I think I should like a cup of coffee. Would you two ladies like something?"

"No, thank you," I said with a small smile. Myron walked away stiff-legged. They weren't getting any younger, and I hated that they had to come all this way from Savannah.

"Carrie Jo, you have to forgive Myron. This really hurts his heart, and he's as ashamed as I am about Mia's behavior. I don't know what's gotten into her. Well, maybe I do." Alice didn't beat about the bush—she never had as long as I'd known her. I sat back in my seat and listened. Alice had a thick southern accent but spoke perfect English, except for the occasional "y'all."

"When Myron and I first married, like many young couples we expected to have a large family. We do love children so, but after a few years of marriage we began to suspect that was not going to happen for us. I went to our family physician and then other doctors, including some fertility specialists, and they confirmed our fears. Having a baby would be medically impossible for us." She tapped her manicured fingernail on the arm of the couch, taking a moment to think about what to say next.

"I cannot describe how difficult that was to hear. But we did not allow it to dissuade us from parenting and decided to adopt Mia. Carrie Jo, she had such a sweet little face and a big laugh that filled the room and our hearts. We instantly fell in love with her. She was so young when we took her home, barely two years old—we had every intention of telling her about the adoption when she got older, but the day never came. We put it off, making excuses, and then she got sick. Mia had come home from Egypt with some kind of fever. As she got sicker, her organs began to fail. The doctors recommended a blood transfusion. Healthy blood would boost her immune system, so naturally they came to us for blood donations. We couldn't donate. Mia has a rare blood type, and we couldn't help her. Anyway, it all worked out. They found the blood they needed, and Mia got better. But of course she had questions."

"I never even knew she was sick."

Alice lowered her eyes and shook her head. "She did not want anyone around; that was especially true after she found out she was adopted. I cannot be sure, but I think that whatever illness she contracted in Egypt—and they were never sure what to call it—affected her thinking. She was not the same girl she had been when she left. The sickness made it worse. Then we had to tell her the truth. She did not take the news well. She called me names, names I had never been called before. It was like someone flipped a switch inside her head. We tried to get her help, but she could not wait to leave us. As soon as she got healthy, she moved out of our house and barely spoke to us. She even began calling us Alice and Myron."

My heart broke for Alice. Why was Mia being so unreasonable? Her adoptive family was kind and loving, even if they hadn't been able to tell her the truth sooner. "I'm sorry, so sorry."

"I am not exactly sure what she did after that, but she mentioned in one of her few emails that she intended to come to Mobile and that you would be here. I was happy because I thought perhaps she would talk to you."

"She never did, Alice. I did not know any of this." But I began to put two and two together. Mia was the best researcher I knew. She would have found out her parentage in less than a month. The girl had connections everywhere. She must have believed, somehow, that she had a right to Calpurnia's fortune. She had said as much the night of the attack. "Knowing Mia, she'd want to find her birth parents. Did she say anything about them? Has she found them?"

"I do not know, Carrie Jo. Obviously, all of this has her unhinged. Now she has attacked you, and you were her best friend. Please forgive her. Forgive me." Alice stifled a sob, and I flew to her side and put my arm around her.

"It's going to be okay, I promise. Mia will get the help she needs now." I squeezed her shoulders to reassure her.

"Miss Jardine?" I looked up to see Detective Simmons standing nearby. "I'm here to take Mia Reed into custody. Got a call from Myron Reed. Do you know anything about this?"

"Hello, Detective. This is Mia's mother, Alice Reed. She and Mr. Reed have convinced their daughter to talk to you. I don't know if questioning Mia right now will help you with your investigation. It appears she has some type of mental problem, something that wasn't there before."

"Be that as it may, I've got no choice but to bring her to the precinct, at least to get her picture and fingerprints. After that, it's up to the district attorney where she goes. Where is she, ma'am?"

"My husband is bringing her down now. But please, do you have to handcuff her?"

"Yes, I'm afraid I do. I'll be as discreet as I can, though."

I heard the elevator ding and saw Myron step out holding Mia's hand. She looked deflated, empty, her vivacious personality hidden beneath a layer of dark depression. I had known her since school and had never known her to go a day without makeup. But her hair looked oily, her pale skin sickly. I saw a spark of anger when her dark eyes fell on Alice, but she smiled when she saw me.

"Carrie Jo? What brings you down here? Couldn't wait to see me in handcuffs? That's rich. Real rich since I did what I did for you. That lawyer wanted to hurt you, CJ. I saved you. End of story."

"Mia Reed? You are under arrest for the murder of Hollis Matthews." Detective Simmons snapped the cuffs on a passive Mia. She led her outside and placed her in a waiting police car. Alice began to cry, and Myron put his arm around her.

"I'm sorry, dear. Oh my, I'm sorry." He blinked back tears. "If you will excuse us, Carrie Jo, I think I will take her back to the room, maybe get some rest."

"Of course. I'm just a phone call away. Please call me if you need me." He nodded and led his sobbing wife from the lobby. It was so odd seeing her cry. Alice Reed never displayed emotions like that in public; she was always such a refined lady, so cool and restrained. Mia had broken her heart. I left the lobby behind with a tear in my eye as well. The police car drove down Water Street, and Mia never looked back. As she promised, Detective Simmons didn't turn on her lights or sirens. It was a quiet end to a bad situation. At least I hoped it was. I walked across the street to my car and called Ashland.

"Good morning," he answered warmly.

"Good morning. I've got some news for you. Good news, I think, even though it doesn't feel that way." I told him about Mia's arrest and the events surrounding it. I hadn't realized how sad I was about it all until that moment.

"Well, maybe she will at least get the help she needs and Hollis' family will have some answers. Are you okay?"

"No, I'm not. I think I'll take a couple hours off this morning, maybe go to the library or take a walk. I don't think anything is pressing at the house at the moment."

"That sounds like a good idea. I've got some things to attend to across the bay, but if you need me..."

"I don't. I mean—I need you, but not for this." I cringed as soon as the words were out of my mouth.

Ever the gentleman, he simply said, "If you change your mind, call me. Take all the time you need. Talk to you later."

"Thanks, Ashland." I sat in my car and stared at the Battle House. Such a beautiful place, such a sad day. My phone rang, and I looked down at the screen. It was William. I snorted and tossed the phone on the seat. I had nothing to say to that betrayer. He must have known that Mia was mentally ill, yet he hadn't done a thing to help her. I had no time for him. None at all.

I drove past Cathedral Square and decided I would go to the library. Melting in my car in this impossible heat thinking about the past wouldn't help me understand any of what had just happened. I didn't need to guess; I needed to catch up on my history. Mia knew something I didn't. And as recent history had shown, that was never good. She had a reason to think she was a potential heir to Calpurnia's fortune. I needed to know what that was.

I pulled into the back parking lot of the library and grabbed my purse and research bag. Maybe some answers could be found here. I walked in and savored the smell of old books and the comfortable coolness of effective air conditioning. As they say in Mobile, "Today was hotter than dirt."

Blinking to adjust my eyes to the lighting, I went up the stairs to the reference section. I set my purse and bag on a back table, away from a cluster of college students whispering about a group project. I remembered those days. *Mia, what happened?* My phone rang again, and I scrambled to find it. I'd forgotten to put it on mute. I saw that it was William again and tapped the ignore button. The voicemail notification dinged, and I slid the phone back in my pocket and began walking down the reference aisles. Archived newspapers and perhaps shipping records would be a good place to start. I spotted a nearby kiosk and began to type.

Let's see, the Mobile Press Register—that's what I need. Hmm...year? 1850. I scanned the headlines. This wasn't going to work. Then I remembered reading that Calpurnia had disappeared in September. I clicked on the month of September and didn't have to click too much more. The first few headlines read, "Officials Search for Missing Heiress," "Cottonwood Girl Disappears" and finally, "Sheriff Fears Missing Debutante is Dead." I read the first article.

Mobile, AL
September 13, 1850

Saturday night, Sheriff Samuel J. Rice visited local plantation Seven Sisters and took account of a missing girl, Calpurnia Cottonwood, daughter of Mr. Jeremiah Cottonwood and the late Mrs. Christine Cottonwood. Miss Cottonwood is sixteen years of age, approximately five feet seven inches tall with brown hair. She may be in the company of a dark-skinned Negro that goes by the name Monticello or Muncie. A reward of $1,000 is being offered for the return of both Miss Cottonwood and the runaway slave. Please contact the sheriff's department with any information about their whereabouts.

That's it? The articles after that one didn't tell me much more. It was as if she really did disappear into thin air. I spent the next couple of hours scrolling through the articles, still not finding much of anything. I decided to switch gears. I began scanning through dozens of bills of lading. I had no way of knowing the exact date Muncie—Janjak—had arrived in Mobile, but I could guess. He probably arrived between 1838 and 1840. These records were heartbreaking. One that really stood out was a bill of lading from the William and Ivy Slave Trading Company of Virginia. Six slaves, including four children, and one free man—all with proper English names like Richard and William. No mention of Monticello or Muncie. Certainly nothing about Janjak. I leaned back in the chair. *Why am I here? I have at least one journal that I haven't read yet, and trying to find Muncie here is like looking for a needle in a haystack.*

Still, there was one more thing I could look up. I typed "slave ships" and "Haiti" into the library's search engine. *Wow! Quite a few hits.* I narrowed it down to the years I thought might be correct. There were four ships that had arrived from

Port-au-Prince, and each listed children on the bill of lading. My heart sank. Such sadness. I sat back in the chair again, wondering what to search for next. I flipped through my notebook. I'd written myself some questions a few weeks ago. Now was as good a time as any to ferret out some answers. I scanned through my handwritten list.

Search the obituaries for Jeremiah Cottonwood, Christine Cottonwood, Isla Beaumont and Louis Beaumont.

I could scratch off Louis Beaumont. Poor handsome, honest Uncle Louis. He hadn't deserved his fate, but we knew what had happened to him now, sadly. I was looking forward to seeing him laid to rest properly.

I typed in "Jeremiah Cottonwood" and "obituary."

August 23, 1853—Died at Seven Sisters on the evening of the 23rd, Mr. Jeremiah Cottonwood, aged 52. Mr. Cottonwood succumbed to death after an accidental fall from his horse on Conception Street. His remains will be interred at the Cottonwood Mausoleum August 27th at 12 o'clock noon. Friends and members of his extended family are respectfully invited to attend the burial service by Rev. England.

I scribbled furiously, making note of the day and time. As we suspected, he was buried on the property in the mausoleum we'd discovered and just three years after Calpurnia disappeared. Excited now to have some progress, I typed in "Isla Beaumont" and "obituary." Nothing. *Okay, try again.* "Isla Grant" and "obituary." Nothing. I was surprised...Isla was an unusual name, even for the 1850s. I typed in "Isla" and "obituary." Nothing except a baby who had passed after a few days of life in the 1870s. So our Isla hadn't died in Mobile.

A young woman like Isla would have found a husband, right? Maybe Captain Garrett?

I stared at the screen for a moment and then typed in "David Garrett" and "obituary."

June 4, 1860—Died in this city on Tuesday evening last, of a gunshot wound in the back, David M. Garrett, Captain of the Delta Queen. He died in what is regarded as good health. Captain Garrett was an explorer and businessman and was attended to the grave by members of his crew and other friends. He was a gentleman of talent and a citizen of commendable habits and propriety of deportment. Though no relative was near to mourn at his grave, he was not alone or laid to rest with strangers. Warm friends attended him, in heart-felt sorrow, to his last resting place at Magnolia Cemetery.

My heart fell in my chest. He'd proved a villain, or at least a betrayer, but I was hoping for a mention of a wife or a female attendant, just on the off chance that Calpurnia had left with him as Muncie had hoped. *Where are you, Callie?*

One more time. I typed in "Christine Cottonwood" and "obituary." Immediately, an entry appeared.

April 7th, 1850—Died on the 7th, Mrs. Christine Beaumont Cottonwood, wife of Jeremiah Cottonwood and daughter of Robert and Marie Beaumont of Birmingham, at 32 years of age.

Mrs. Cottonwood was a lady of many attractive graces and worthy virtues, remarkable for the earnestness of her friendships, her kindness to her fellow citizens and her large circle of kindred, whom the loss most affects.

She leaves behind a devoted husband and a loving daughter. Mrs. Cottonwood was laid to rest in the Cottonwood Mausoleum in witness of her family.

No mention of the baby Angelique? I scribbled down some notes and stuffed my notebook back in my research bag. I walked back out into the sunshine, contemplating all that I'd just learned. It wasn't surprising that they all died comparatively young. People did die younger in those days. Still no Calpurnia, but I'd done enough for the day. I remembered what Ashland had said about TD, about needing Detra Ann's help in mending fences.

It was time to eat a little crow. I sat in my steamy Honda, waiting for the air conditioning to offer some relief from the wilting heat. I dialed Detra Ann's number and crossed my fingers as the phone rang.

"Hi, Detra Ann? This is Carrie Jo Jardine. I was wondering, are you free this afternoon or maybe tomorrow? I'd like to talk to you about Seven Sisters."

"Oh. Hi, Carrie Jo. Yes, I'm free this afternoon. Around 4:30? Should I meet you at the house?"

I looked at my watch. That gave me a few hours. "Yes, that's perfect. I'll see you then." I hung up the phone and drove to the mansion. *This should be interesting.*

Chapter 11

My knees wobbled a bit as I reached above my head to straighten one of the crystals on the chandelier. Being on a ladder was not my favorite activity—I hated heights—but the possibility that TD's crew would lift this chandelier into place without fixing it drove me crazy. Under normal circumstances the contractor would have spotted the problem immediately, but he wasn't around today. Not that we talked much anymore. If I knew anything about contract labor, it was not to take anything for granted when the boss was away. As cautiously as I could, my shaking hands unwound the strings and the shard dangled free. I breathed a sigh of relief and prepared to ease back down to the safe ground.

"What are you doing?" The ladder shook under me. I froze and gasped for breath, as if that would steady me. "Oh my God, I didn't mean to startle you. Here, let me hold the ladder." It was Detra Ann, a bit early for our appointment.

I climbed down as quickly as I could with a nervous laugh. "You move like a ninja! I didn't hear you come in, and normally every sound in this room echoes; it's such a huge space."

"I'm really sorry about that. I have on heels; I would have thought you'd heard me coming in." She laughed, and I could tell she was nervous too.

"No problem. I guess my concentration was focused on getting that crystal untangled. I didn't hear a thing."

She looked around in awe of the room. "It's looking amazing. I have to say that I'm really impressed at how much you all have accomplished in just a few months. This is simply amazing."

"Thank you. We do make a pretty good team. Ashland has the brains, TD has the know-how, and I know the history. It's all worked out, thankfully." She nodded in agreement.

"You said you wanted to talk to me. I'm hoping that means you've changed your mind about having a ball here?"

"Nothing is off the table, Detra Ann, but I'm surprised that you'd still want to have a ball here after all the rumors you've likely heard about ghosts. That hasn't put you off?"

"Oh, come on now. In the world of marketing, having a ghost or two is only a plus. And you don't have to pretend with me; I know something happened here. Is anyone ever going to tell me what that was?"

I didn't know what to make of that. From what I had heard from Rachel, Detra Ann had told the interns about what TD saw that night, but maybe she didn't know everything. I had no idea. "Now who's pretending? Surely TD told you everything." I couldn't explain it, but I suddenly felt the hair standing up on my arms. I looked around the room, thinking someone had joined us. There was no furniture to hide behind here in the ballroom, but no doors had opened either. If anyone was here, I couldn't see them. Detra Ann looked around suspiciously and then stared at me. She was probably thinking I was crazy or at least melodramatic.

"Can we just talk without all the snark? For whatever reason, I do think we got off on the wrong foot. I'm Ashland's friend, but it is Terrence Dale that I am interested in. I'm not your competition. So can we try?"

Detra Ann's directness brought me back to reality, but my need to leave the room grew by the second. "Sorry. Sure, let's talk about it. I think I know the perfect place." I cast a worried eye around the room and led her to the Rose Garden porch. It was another scorcher out, but there was plenty of shade on the porch and an oversized ceiling fan with blades that looked like palm leaves. And it would get us out of the house.

We sat at one of the tables, and I turned the fan on high. Detra Ann looked so neat and polished in a light pink summer suit, and I felt underdressed in my white capris, blue and white checkered top and white tennis shoes. Her long dark hair was perfectly brushed and captured in place with a clear ponytail elastic, and her hairstyle put my sweaty, messy bun to shame. "I wanted to talk to you because I've come to a dead end, historically speaking. I agree, we did get off on the wrong foot, and that was at least partly my fault. I am sorry for that. I would like to be friends, and I think we can do some good here at Seven Sisters."

"I am so happy to hear that." Her hand flew to her chest and she smiled. "I agree. I know I come off as pushy sometimes, but I have five brothers. I guess being pushy and outspoken is a learned behavior."

"Wow, five? That must have been an interesting childhood."

"Oh yes, indeed. But thankfully my mom and I were very close, and I have a ton of girl cousins. There was no end to girly activities for me to participate in." We talked a little more about her family and her interest in promoting Mobile businesses. She didn't ask me about my family, and I didn't offer.

"So what did TD tell you about the party? He had to have told you something—one of the interns said you asked her if she'd seen a ghost."

Looking relieved, Detra Ann leaned forward in her cushioned chair. "I can't tell you how shook up TD was that night. He came to my house at two in the morning, and he must have drunk a six-pack before he drove over because he was loaded. At first, he couldn't stop talking about the Moonlight Garden, about you and Ashland, but he wasn't making much sense. He said something about the wind and a secret place in the maze, but when he sobered up the next day, he didn't want to tell me anything. I've never seen him so emotional. Restoring the Moonlight Garden had been such a dream for him; he had put everything into it, and now he barely talks about it. It's like he wants to forget it completely. I asked around because I wasn't getting any answers from TD and I knew better than to ask Ashland. He's never hidden his disdain for the supernatural. I have to admit that I'm happy we're talking about this now. Will you please tell me what happened? I'd like to be able to help the man I love."

My sympathetic heart decided then and there that I would tell her the truth and let the chips fall where they may. She needed to hear it if she was going to help TD recover. If it were Ashland, I would want to know. "All right, but some of what I'm going to tell you might sound incredible—even impossible. I'll tell you what I can, but I'm not an expert in ghosts or anything."

"From the little that TD told me, I thought you were some kind of ghost hunter. Did you see them before coming to Seven Sisters?"

A nervous laugh escaped my lips, "Uh, no, I'm not. At least I wasn't before I got here. I've had a few dreams over the years that were about certain places, but I don't have psychic powers or anything like that. There are times when I feel things, like just a few minutes ago in the ballroom."

"Oh, I felt uncomfortable too. But I didn't see anything, did you?" Her blue eyes were wide.

"No, like I said, I don't normally see anything, at least not when I am awake. But that night in the garden was different. We all saw her, the ghost—even TD. You see..." I related the story as best I could to her, and her plump pink lips parted in amazement as I told her about our furious dig and the discovery of the lost treasure.

At some time during the story, she'd kicked off her shoes, and her feet were tucked underneath her at an angle. We looked like two sorority sisters sharing secrets on the porch of Seven Sisters. As I recalled the supernatural experience, I remembered how cold I had felt, how the evil wind had disturbed the fallen leaves and flowers. In my mind's eye I could see Isla appearing alive except for her missing skirt hem and feet. I could easily recall her losing all color of life and turning ash-gray like one of the statues in the garden. I shivered.

"And you swear this is the truth—you aren't pulling my leg at all?" Her eyes narrowed suspiciously, and I didn't blame her. I'd be suspicious too if I didn't know what I knew, hadn't seen what I'd seen. I left out the part about Henri Devecheaux; there was no sense in bringing him into my story unless she asked. I had a warm spot in my heart for the bumbling ghost hunter. He'd disappeared, probably in an effort to distance himself from the house and all its occupants.

"No, I'm not. Everything I have told you is the absolute truth. I hope you believe me."

"I believe you, Carrie Jo. I believe you saw what you say you saw. I believe TD saw her too." Detra Ann chewed on her lower lip, thinking deeply about what she had just heard. "I have to admit that I'm glad I left early. I would have screamed my head off if I'd seen anything. I'm kind of a wimp when it comes to stuff like that." In a quieter voice, she asked, "Have you seen anything else since then?"

"Nothing like that night," I said. "Still want to hold a ball here?"

She laughed nervously. "Well, if we did, I don't think that's the story I'd tell."

I breathed a sigh of relief. "Thanks for not laughing at me or saying you don't believe me. This is so crazy, who would make that up?"

"Girl, I'm a true Mobilian. We don't hide the skeletons in our closets, and we don't laugh at the idea of ghosts. It's just not good manners."

"Thanks, Detra Ann."

She leaned forward spontaneously and squeezed my hands. "However, I don't think TD is as willing as I am to accept the fact that the dead sometimes aren't all that dead. He's really struggling, but at least I know what I'm dealing with now. I have an idea that might help him."

"Really? What's that?"

"I'll take him to church."

"What?" I laughed.

"No, really, I think it will help. TD is a solid guy; he just needs to get grounded again. I'll take him to my church, Cottage Hill Methodist."

"You think a church visit will do it?"

"Not just a visit. It might take a while, but yeah, that's what I think he needs. Don't worry about TD. Leave him to me. I'll get him back on track."

I totally believed she was committed to helping him, and as I'd suspected, she had designs on him. She had even said she loved him. Terrence Dale may as well surrender now and come peacefully because when a woman like Detra Ann sets her mind on something, she gets it. I admired her, and I was glad to know that he had someone in his corner. Regardless of how things had gone with us, I hoped for the best for him.

"That's great to hear. I've been worried about him."

"Well, he's going to be okay. Thank you for telling me the truth. Now what can I help you with? You said earlier that you were at a dead end. What can I do?"

Thankful that we were working together at last, I said, "I promised Ashland that I would help him find Calpurnia Cottonwood, the missing heiress who used to live here. My research led me to a steamboat captain named David Garrett. There was some evidence that he might have been involved in the girl's disappearance. I was hoping that maybe you'd know something about this Captain Garrett. I think his boat was the Delta Queen, used to run up and down the Mobile River in the 1850s, delivering cotton, and there was some gambling on board too. Have you ever heard of him?"

"Ever heard of him? My stars! My mother is an expert on David Garrett—I heard plenty of stories about him growing up. She even has a small oil painting of the captain, or so she believes, on her mantelpiece. As far as Calpurnia Cottonwood goes, I've never heard anything that put those two together, but I wouldn't put it past him. The captain had an eye for the ladies, especially wealthy ones, according to the reports. Is it any wonder that he was shot in the back by a woman?"

"It was a woman who shot him? Do you know who she was?"

"No, I don't recall her name. She was arrested for it but somehow got away. She disappeared, and nobody ever heard from her again. Nobody made much fuss, though. Who's going to cry for a guy who made a career out of deflowering debutantes and scamming their families for money to keep it quiet? If he hadn't been so ridiculously handsome and charming, they would have strung him up after the first time it happened."

"Who was that?"

"One of the Bellingrath girls, the middle one. That was before they moved to Mobile from Castleberry. She was the mother of Walter Bellingrath, the gentleman who created Bellingrath Gardens with his wife. Now what was his mother's name? I can't remember, but apparently she caught David Garrett's eye during a picnic lunch by the river. He bounded off the boat and eventually right into her heart, but not before her father did his best to prevent those two from getting too close. Old Mr. Bellingrath knew a scoundrel when he saw one. He was a tough old dude—he fought the Indians in Texas when he was a young man, and he'd made quite a bit of money through trading in the territory. That's the Louisiana Territory." I nodded, hoping she'd quickly get to the point. "Well, anyway, by the time he figured out that Captain Garrett had been shimmying up the trellis into his daughter's room, it was too late. The deed had been done. In those days, it was perfectly legal to have a man arrested for taking such liberties, but that almost guaranteed that the young woman and her family name would forever be tarnished. Of course, Garrett offered to marry the girl if Mr. Bellingrath paid him the dowry he was asking for, but the old man blew the roof. He wasn't going to give Garrett a fortune after he'd dishonored his daughter. Garrett supposedly laughed in his face and said, "I'll just take the money, then. I'm sure your daughter will find a suitable replacement for me when I'm gone."

"You're joking! What a horrible thing to do!"

"I know. Aren't we all glad that we don't live in the 1850s? So Mr. Bellingrath gave up his fortune, but he didn't give up his daughter. Unfortunately for him, Sharon—that was her name—couldn't keep a secret. She cried and cried and blamed her father for sending her sweetheart away. Eventually word got out, and the family moved back to Castleberry for quite a few years. Sharon supposedly later married a clerk who worked in one of her father's businesses, but no marriage license was ever found. Now we have found a birth certificate, and of course the baby was Walter Bellingrath, who eventually moved back to Mobile and established Belle Camp with his wife. Later it became Bellingrath Gardens."

"So Walter Bellingrath could have been Garrett's son?"

"Possibly, quite possibly."

"Could she have shot Garrett? Is that what happened?"

"No, I don't think so. Sharon Bellingrath didn't do much socializing after her public shaming, but the captain kept his game going. She was definitely not the only one. There was a young opera singer named Trixie Cartwright—a stage name, I'm sure—that he fancied for some time, but I don't know much about her."

My mind swam with the information she'd shared with me, but there was still nothing about Calpurnia.

"Oh, there is one more thing. He had a sister...wow, her name escapes me at the moment. She was a younger sister that he was quite devoted to. She didn't live with him; she had some kind of illness that kept her in and out of the hospital. But he saw her every time he came to Mobile, brought her gifts. My mother has a copy of a letter he wrote her. Would you like me to email you a scan later?"

"Yes! Would you? I would love to see that. And if you know anything else about Calpurnia—anything at all—please let me know. I'd like to find her before my work here is done. I can't even imagine leaving this place without knowing what happened to her."

"It's been quite a mystery for so many years. I honestly hope you do find her, but don't get your hopes up. So many people have searched for her and have met with sad fates. You're such a nice person, and I'd hate for something to happen to you."

Suddenly, the fan that spun above us stopped. The blades didn't just slow down, they came to a screeching halt as if an invisible hand had grabbed them and held them still. Both of us looked up. Detra Ann's eyes were wide with fear, but to my surprise, I was just mad. "Whatever," I said to the empty air above me. "I'll walk you out to your car, Detra Ann." We didn't go back through the house but hopped off the porch and walked down the driveway.

"Oh my God. What just happened?"

"I couldn't tell you," I confessed with a shrug.

"But I thought the ghost, Isla, was gone."

"Me too, but we don't know that was a ghost. And if it was, we don't know it was Isla."

"So there's more than one now?"

"I wouldn't doubt it. Please don't let word of this get out. It would ruin Ashland's dream of bringing his family home back to life, and I think if we found Calpurnia it would end. Don't ask me why, but I truly believe it would. That's why I have to."

"Yes, I can see that. Okay, I'm going to get all the info I can. I'll email that over ASAP. Is your work email the one I should use?"

I nodded. "That's perfect."

"I'll send anything else I find too. You have my word that I won't mention any of this, but you have to do the same. TD doesn't need to know about what happened with the fan or anything else. It would just freak him out worse."

"You've got a deal." I reached my hand out to shake hers, but instead she hugged me and smiled. "No handshakes! We hug in Mobile. You might as well get used to it. You're one of us now."

"Well, for a little while," I said.

She smiled. "I have no supernatural powers, but this I can predict—you're utterly and completely hooked. And not just on the house. You're a part of the story now, Carrie Jo. Part of Ashland's story, and a part of Mobile too. Once Mobile gets in your blood, you'll never be the same." She tossed her briefcase on the passenger seat and got into her light blue Mercedes.

I smiled at her and gave her a little wave as she drove away.

I knew she was absolutely right. I was part of the story now, but how would it end?

Chapter 12

Going home, I had so much to think about. I left Seven Sisters with an incomplete checklist of daily tasks, which I hated, but there was always tomorrow. As I drove down the bumpy road in my faithful Honda, I thought about my conversation with Detra Ann. I couldn't be happier that we were working together, and I couldn't wait to get that email from her. Off in the distance, grayish-black clouds hung heavy in the sky, rolling in from Mobile Bay. The threatening puffs looked impressive against the bright green leaves of the trees.

I planned on getting into the last of the journals and taking some notes that night. I felt like we were teetering on the edge of the truth, but that truth—in whatever form it would come—had not yet manifested.

I turned right into the driveway and waved at Bette, who was at her kitchen sink washing dishes. She waved back with a gloved hand. I made a mental note to make some time for my friend as soon as possible. Bienville didn't greet me as he often did, and I assumed it was because Bette was home now. That was okay. I liked having a part-time cat. I was in no way responsible enough to have a pet of my own.

A crack of thunder hastened my steps up the wooden staircase, and I looked out over the tree line below, again impressed with the sights and smells of the impending storm. Oddly enough, I loved storms as long as I didn't have to stand outside in one. Once inside, I unplugged my laptop to prevent an unwanted shock. I had so much material saved there, and I couldn't afford to lose it from a random lightning strike. I opened it up to check my email. Nope, nothing yet. But it hadn't even been an hour. *Be patient, CJ.* I hung up my purse and kicked off my shoes. I'd get a shower after the storm, and I didn't have to go out for supper. I had leftover wonton soup in my kitchenette. That would be the perfect dinner for an evening of reading, researching and hopefully some dreaming.

I had just pulled an oversized t-shirt over my head and slid into some yoga pants when someone knocked on my door. Puzzled, I paused before walking to the window and peeking downstairs. I saw Ashland's car and couldn't help but smile.

"Hey, come on in before you get caught in that storm." As if God were emphasizing my warning, lightning streaked across the Mobile sky, and I could see the rain approaching in the distance. He stepped inside, looking distracted and wet. "Oh no, I didn't even notice. You're drenched already! Let me get you a towel."

"That would be great," he said with a chuckle. "I'm obviously not as fast a runner as I used to be."

"Where are you coming from? The boat?" I called from the bathroom as I dug for the last clean towel. I'd have to do laundry ASAP. I padded back to him and handed him the towel. His blond hair was dripping wet. "Or maybe you swam from the Bay?"

He laughed. "I sure look like it, don't I? No, I've been downtown at Matthews and Ladner."

"Oh, good. Did they finally give you all your files?" I knew he'd been after the law firm to turn over everything that pertained to him. They were hesitant at first, and Ladner, the surviving partner, didn't even want to work with Ashland's new attorney. But naturally, Ashland persisted and got what he wanted.

"Yes, I got most of it yesterday, but I just got the last pack of paperwork this afternoon. You won't believe what I found." He was holding a folder, and his smile was almost electric.

"Here, sit on a barstool in the kitchen and tell me about it while I dry your hair. Were we right? Did Hollis know about the necklace?" I rubbed Ashland's hair vigorously with the towel and then rubbed his strong, broad shoulders in an attempt to dry his white button-down shirt. It wasn't working, but I enjoyed every minute of it. Finally, I tossed the towel over a chair and sat down. "What did you find? I can tell you're dying to tell me, and I'm dying to know! I heard something pretty amazing today myself."

He ran his hand through his messy hair and sat at the table with me. "Some of this might be hard to believe. But once you know everything, I think you'll have to admit I did pretty good."

"Okay, okay. You're the king of research, now spill it."

He opened his sheaf and pulled out some papers. Most were copies, old copies, from the look of it. I flipped on the light because the storm had made the room as dark as midnight.

"How many living children did Christine and Jeremiah Cottonwood have?" he asked. "Just the one, Calpurnia, right?"

"That's right." I didn't know where he was going with this, so I listened as patiently as I could.

"Take a look at this." He slid me a copy of a marriage license, dated March 13, 1867, in faded ink. The text read: "The State of Alabama and the County of Mobile Probate Court. To any of the State Judges or to any Licensed Minister of the Gospel or to any Justice of the Peace of the said County.

Know ye that you are hereby authorized to join together in the Bonds of Holy Matrimony..." I peered closer to read the names, "Edward H. Tulley and Karah Lahoma Cottonwood."

"What is this? Some cousin of Calpurnia's? Maybe Jeremiah's brother's child?"

"Nope. She's not." His face beamed with excitement.

"Well, who is she?"

He dug in his folder and pulled out a photo of the couple, seated in a studio. A tall young man stood behind a couch, unsmiling, with perfectly smooth dark hair and dark eyes. Seated on the couch was the bride, her hair piled on her head, the dress collar cinched around her long neck, a hint of a smile at the corner of her lips.

I stood up and carried the photo into the living room, turning on the desk lamp. I ransacked the desk drawer for the magnifying glass. Oh, that familiar smile and the shape of the neck! Even her piles of hair made me think of Calpurnia. It wasn't her, but the resemblance was striking.

"What? Who is this, Ashland?"

"Meet Karah Lahoma Cottonwood Tulley, of our Cottonwoods. I think she's Calpurnia's long-lost sister."

"But how can that be? I mean, there's no record of a living child other than Callie."

"No, but unlike the other children, there are no death records, not even a mention of her death in the family bible. Don't you think that's kind of suspect? I do believe this is the baby that Calpurnia heard crying the night her mother died. Remember, she was surprised to learn that the baby died because she'd heard it crying sometime late that night. Somebody must have taken the baby away."

"Or been ordered to remove it. I wouldn't put it past Old Jeremiah to want to get rid of her. He didn't want another girl, and he sure didn't want to share that fortune, even if he couldn't find it."

"Yes, but from what you say and what I have read, it's more likely that Mr. Cottonwood would have wanted the baby dead."

"Ah, yes, but Jeremiah was a coward, except when it came to abusing his wife and daughter. He would have never done the deed himself. Just like Ann-Sheila."

"Who?"

I shook my head, thinking of the poor slave who drowned herself in the river. "It's not important right now. I'm just saying that he would have ordered one of his slaves to do it, probably Stokes or Early." I paced the floor, the wheels turning like crazy in my mind. "But Hooney, she would have intervened. I'm sure of it. She cared about Christine. It would have been easy for her to have that baby hidden away somewhere."

"It's hard to imagine how it all happened, but this photo seems like good proof to me. Somehow that baby lived. I wish we knew more."

"Well, there's nothing to do but have a nap. Maybe a nap with that photo will trigger something. It's hit or miss, but it's worth a shot."

"No way, CJ. I won't let you do that. It's too dangerous, especially with all we know now. I've only scratched the surface of what my supposed friend, Hollis Matthews, knew. I don't know how far down this rabbit hole goes."

"Literary references are appreciated, but you can't stop me from dreaming, Ashland." Lighting popped near the house, and the lights went off. Thunder shook the dishes in my kitchen cabinet. We both jumped and then nervously laughed at ourselves.

He said, "I'm not trying to stop you from dreaming. I just wish you'd dream about me once in a while." He stood close to me, his face the picture of seriousness, his shirt and hair almost dry now.

"Why should I dream about you? You're here, right now, aren't you? That's better than a dream." I reached out and touched his chest, putting the palm of my hand over his heart. Through the thin cotton shirt, I could feel his heart beating strong and evenly.

"Yes, I am here," he answered in a hoarse whisper.

I stepped closer. We were so close now that there was barely any space between us. My breath was coming faster, my heart pounded, my pulse raced. With a tilt of my head, I gazed into his blue eyes and whispered, "I am here too."

He took my face in his hands and kissed me. This was no "Bye, see you later" kiss. We weren't two teenagers parked in the woods after the prom but two adults who, until this point, had managed to keep our hands off one another. We kissed again, and I felt the weight of my hair fall around my shoulders as he slid my hair out of its ponytail. I got the feeling that Ashland wasn't leaving, and I didn't want him to. He paused and looked at me; his eyes sparkled with desire, his unspoken question obvious. I didn't speak a word but instead replied with a kiss. Yes, I wanted him to stay.

And he did.

Chapter 13

Neither one of us fell asleep, but we lay in the dark together for a long time before Ashland slipped away. He took his stack of paperwork with him except for the photo, which I convinced him to leave behind. I posted the picture of Karah next to Calpurnia's on my dry-erase board and sat in my curved chair clad in my t-shirt, my body half-wrapped in a sheet. The nearby streetlight cast a strange yellow glow on the board. I stared at the two faces looking back at me from antiquity. They wouldn't pass for identical twins—Karah's eyes didn't have the downward slant of Calpurnia's—but I could well imagine they might be sisters. Definitely related in some way. Their eye color could be similar. It was hard to tell with just a copy of an antique black and white photograph and a photo of an oil painting. I looked more carefully, taking note of the differences and similarities.

Their lips, full and bow-shaped, the same. Both had high cheekbones, but Karah's forehead was wider, like Christine's. Similarities were there, but it would be hard to know for sure without solid evidence. Here was another question: if Karah knew she was a Cottonwood, as the marriage license seemed to suggest, why didn't she come forward and claim her birthright, claim Seven Sisters? What had kept her away? I sighed. *Another mystery, like I need another one. Okay, no more distractions tonight.* I had to get my mind back on my task here—finding Calpurnia. Last I knew, she confessed to Muncie that she wanted to leave. But to where and with whom?

I picked up the journal and hunkered down in the chair. Thankfully the power had flickered back on, and I switched on the lamp. I ran my fingers over the cover of the journal and opened it to my bookmark. *Talk to me, Calpurnia. Give me some kind of clue! Where are you?*

I sighed, closed my eyes to quiet myself and began to read...

Dear Diary,

Pichon's Emporium delivered new dresses to the house today; some were mine, and the rest belonged to Mother. How easily I can call to remembrance her laughter when ordering those items. She'd given Mr. Pichon's unfriendly daughter her measurements with a smile, promising me that she would indeed regain her trim figure after the baby arrived. I didn't care what size her waist was—Mother's beauty was impossible to hide, and I had told her so. Now those dresses would never be worn, although Cousin Isla would undoubtedly ask me for them. My Cousin has a Persuasive Manner, and Truthfully I rarely refused her, but on this subject I would be unmovable. Nobody would wear Mother's dresses, not as long as there was breath in my body. I could not bear to see Isla preening about in them as if she were truly the Lady of the House. She's already taken to ordering our meals, even purchasing supplies, and she recently had the houseboys rearranging the furniture in the Ladies' Parlor. These privileges had been given to her by my Father, I supposed, and I did not challenge her.

For these things I care not, as I do not plan to remain at Seven Sisters. Let Isla have her little victories over me, like telling Hooney I had not eaten or mentioning to my Father that I had not accepted Mrs. Meadows' call. I had long abandoned the idea that Isla held any love for me. She was not a True Friend—like Muncie.

But she will never wear Mother's dresses!

How oddly reassuring it had been to receive the packages, when just a few weeks ago I could have never dreamed that I would welcome such a delivery. Indeed to receive such an intimate package would have sunk my soul like an anchor into the depths of darkest despair. But this had not happened.

As I opened the box lid and lifted away the tissue paper from the cream and peach dress, it was as if my Own Dear Mother had sent this gift to remind me to remain strong and hopeful. I had ignored Hooney's yellow-eyed stare and removed the sumptuous fabric, hugging it as if it were my Dearest One. I spread it across the pillows of my bed and lay beside it, rubbing the fabric with my fingers. I hummed "La Mere," feeling sleepy but happy. Hooney murmured a prayer, most certainly about me and my Addled Mind, and left me alone to my musings.

Mother could never escape Seven Sisters now. I could not help her, but she wanted me to be free. She wanted me to run, as far and as fast as I could. That was the message I received from her dress box. I love you, Mother!

Now, I have taken Great Care to behave as if All is Well again. I ordered a bath and asked Hannah to fix my hair. I greeted my Cousin with a smile and even inquired about her health. She chattered like the day we first met. My Cousin considered herself to be Crafty and Intelligent, but she had no idea what I had planned. I smiled through her retelling of a bit of gossip she had picked up from our neighbor and her friend, Ocie Chastang.

"How amusing," I commented as she continued her tale. Apparently some newcomer to the Mobile Social Scene discovered that the local "parlor fan language" was quite different from the fan languages used in her home parish. Miss Louise Holcombe had made a fool of herself in front of an entire new crop of debutantes visiting from Jackson County. Isla laughed and laughed, and I did my very best to echo her amusement.

She cajoled me to come out and accompany her and visit with Ocie. She told me I looked lovely in my new dress and remarked, "I am sure that all the Gentlemen in Mobile County will be heartbroken when they discover you are to marry Mr. Langdon." She leaned back against the upholstered chair, her blue cotton dress—my blue cotton dress—surrounding her tiny frame like a blue cloud. She told me she was Quite Jealous that I should marry and move away, leaving her in this Great House by herself. "How will I ever manage?" she said with a pout. She feigned sadness, but she did not fool me. I knew that she did not feel it. I suspected that Isla Beaumont had never felt sad a day in her life. She never cried. Not for her Mother or mine. Not for Baby Angelique. Not a tear for Uncle Louis beyond dabbing a handkerchief to her dry eyes the day he disappeared. Muncie had tried to warn me, but I had refused to listen. Now I knew.

At the very least she had kept my Great Secret and never revealed to Father that I had spirited away a Collection of Letters from My Captain. Yes, at least there was that.

Tonight, as I prepared for bed, I examined again his latest letter. How his written words tug at my heartstrings like a violin master plucks at his instrument! Apparently some fiend—some Agent of Low Caliber—has shared the news that I am to marry. Read his words to me...

Were I not a Gentleman of the South, how rudely I would lambast Your Proposed Husband to his Bride, but Alas, Madam, I am such. Inasmuch as it Pains My Heart, I release you from any Inclinations or Dispositions in regards to myself, knowing that I could never attain the Stature of the Man you are soon scheduled to marry. Forgive My intrusion and think kindly of me, Friend. I will Treasure Our Memories beyond a mere tomorrow.

With fondest farewell,

Captain David Garrett

My hand shook so when I sent my return. I assured the Captain that I had no desire to end our Friendship, that I considered him an Excellent Man and a Dear Friend. I refused to say goodbye, writing this...

Now, my Friend, accept my heart-felt assurance that I continue to Value Our Amiable Acquaintance. That in truth, I have no designs to abandon you. Nay, how much more will I rely upon your Companionship as I navigate these Unknown Waters? I look forward to the Good Day when I may see you Face to Face. I pray that when that day arrives, I will have the Courage necessary to speak my True Heart.

Yours in Friendship,

Calpurnia Cottonwood

My note is winging its way to the Captain now. I pray that I may hear a return soon. What will I say to him? I am determined to speak my heart at last. I want to be His Wife and the wife of no other. For freedom—no, for his Love—I would gladly shed all my earthly trappings, pay whatever price, even lose my inheritance to be by his side. Oh, to see the world! To explore the sights and sound of life beyond my white sepulcher! One more word of encouragement, and I shall run to him with all my strength. I *pray that it is soon—Isla tells me that the Delta Queen shall leave Mobile soon, probably for the rest of the season. He must write to me! I will wait for him!*

How will I pass the time?

Chapter 14

I woke up with a weird startled feeling hanging over me. My phone buzzed on my nightstand—it was Ashland. It was never good when he called before 8 a.m. I pushed my unruly curls out of my face and answered the phone, trying not to sound like someone coming out of a love hangover from a night of passion.

"Dreaming about me?" His question caught me off guard, and I couldn't help but smile.

"Of course, Ashland," I started to lie but added, "well, kind of. I dreamed about Callie." Naturally, he wanted to know all the details, so I relayed what I saw, from the dresses to the notes. He prodded me with questions, and by the end of the conversation, I felt sort of sad. Not about the dream, but about Ashland and me. What would happen to us when the mystery of Calpurnia's whereabouts was solved? What if we never knew what happened? Nothing would be sadder than to discover that Ashland and I truly had nothing in common except for a love of old houses. I finished the conversation with, "Will I see you later?"

"I'm thinking about driving up to Fayette. That's where Karah was from, according to what I've found. It's about four hours away. I was thinking we could ride up and spend the afternoon exploring the library records, stay overnight, come back some time on Sunday. How does that sound?"

I waved my hand in the air in frustration—mostly at myself. My heart said, "Go! Go! Go!" but my brain was shouting, "Not so fast!" I won't even mention what my other parts were saying. "I wish I could say yes, but I better not."

He laughed nervously. "I guess that doesn't sound like much of a date."

"That sounds like the perfect date to me. It's just that I'd like to visit with Myron and Alice before they go home, and I need to do a few things around here that I've been neglecting." Like my laundry, I thought. "How about a rain check?"

"Sure, but I don't know when I'll be driving back to Fayette, Alabama, population 2,400 again."

"I'll take my chances. Besides, I have confidence in you. Keep your eyes open for anything you think might be relevant, and let's talk tonight. I'm dying to know who this sister of Calpurnia's is."

"Yeah, me too."

The pause in the conversation grew. It felt like Ashland had something to say, but he never said whatever was on his mind. "You still there?"

"Yes, I'm here."

Suddenly I regretted my decision. Maybe I should change my mind, pack a bag and head to Fayette for the weekend. But before I could, Bette tapped courteously on my door, giving me the excuse I needed to end the awkward phone call. How could this be? Ashland and I had finally shared an amazing intimate evening, and now I wanted to run the other way. What the hell was wrong with me?

"I better go. Bette's here. Have a safe trip, Ashland. Call me later?"

"Yes, I'll call before bed. Talk to you later."

"Bye." I hung up the phone, trotted to the door and opened it with a smile. "Bette! I feel like I haven't seen you in forever. How are you?"

"I'm very well, thank you! Listen, I brought you a crock of hot cheese grits with some bacon sprinkled on top. I would invite you down to the kitchen, but my gentleman friend decided to sleep on the couch last night. I had extra and I wanted to share. How's my Bienville been behaving?"

"Thank you for the grits!" I accepted the crock, grateful for the worn potholders she passed me with it. Naturally, they were Campbell's Soup Kids quilt blocks. I adored Bette's kitschy kitchen. If I ever had a real home of my own, my kitchen would be every bit as tacky and comforting. "Come on in, Bette." I padded into the kitchen and set the crock on the small table. "He's been a perfect gentleman. He comes and goes, but I forgive him because he's so huggable."

"That sounds a lot like my gentleman friend." I hoped she hadn't noticed that Ashland had stayed longer than normal last night. That would be almost as embarrassing as hearing about Bette's beau "sleeping on the couch."

"Do you plan to do laundry today? I'd like to use the washer and dryer if you don't mind. I'm running out of socks and underwear."

"Sure, you go right ahead. I'm not doing laundry today. Oh, I heard they arrested Mia. Any word on what's next? I figured they'd lock her up in some nuthouse somewhere. The poor girl is delusional, don't you think?"

"Yes, I do. I hope someone helps her, because she's a danger."

"To you, she is. Please be careful, Carrie Jo. I don't want anything to happen to you. You're like another one of my kids—or grandkids. I have gotten attached to you being here."

"Me too, Bette. Thanks for your hospitality and your friendship."

She sniffed and walked to the door. "Have a nice day, dear. And if you see a short, balding man with a noticeable limp leave, please don't judge me." She giggled and waved at me as she walked down the stairs.

I loved Bette and her quirkiness. She was a nice lady. I was happy to see her looking so perky. Not long ago we were fighting for our lives; Mia probably would have killed us both and now it was as if none of it ever happened. What a difference a short time makes!

I poured a glass of orange juice and sat down to enjoy my grits. These quiet moments made everything feel right again. I didn't normally "work" at my kitchen table, but I grabbed the laptop and began typing frantically into my dream journal, recording everything I could for posterity's sake. Of course, I didn't know if I'd ever have a future generation, but just in case. I shivered uncontrollably, then decided to get some coffee. I drank it black; I needed the energy boost, not extra calories. I removed the lid from the thick creamy grits and enjoyed the aroma: butter...cheese...a touch of garlic powder. That was the secret!

Gobbling them as quickly as I could without burning my mouth, I filled up my tummy with cheese grits. Sure, no extra calories there. I put the dish in the sink and ran some water in it. Grits were like wallpaper paste once they dried, impossible to remove without power tools. I scrolled through my phone's contact list and tapped on Alice Reed's name.

We talked for a half-hour. Alice was friendly, but I could hear the sadness in her voice. I understood that. Having a loved one with a mental illness was a heartache that one couldn't explain to anyone who hadn't experienced it. Apparently the Reeds had Mia settled into Mobile Mental Health for the next four weeks for various evaluations. The couple had returned to Savannah to put their house in order. They planned on moving back to the area to be near their daughter during her recovery. As she was technically in the County's custody, she could not leave the state until she went to trial for the death of Hollis Matthews. No way were they going to leave her to fight this battle alone. I admired their fortitude and prayed that one day Mia would come to realize that Alice and Myron were more of a treasure than any sack of jewels or old house could ever be. Alice ended the call by asking me to go see Mia when I could.

"You would be doing us a favor, and I know she wants to see you—you are all she talks about."

I gave her an indefinite maybe before wishing them well.

I took a long, cool shower because the day was shaping up to be another warm one. East Coast living was hot—Mobile had to be the humidity capital of the U.S.—at least of Alabama. I turned on the radio and sang along with Joan Jett. I screeched, "I love rock 'n' roll! Put another dime in the jukebox, baby..." When my concert ended, I dried off, dressed and began sorting my dirty laundry. Luckily for me, the washer and dryer were downstairs so I didn't have to carry everything too far. I put the first load in, tossed in some detergent and walked back upstairs with my empty basket.

My phone was ringing, and out of habit I picked it up without looking at the screen. "Hello?"

"Hey, CJ?" I spun around again, waving my hand at myself in frustration. *What do I do? What do I do?* I didn't want to talk to William. What would I say to him? Besides call him a few choice names. I banged my hand on the counter.

"Yes, this is CJ."

"Don't hang up on me! I've been trying to call you for days. I have to—"

"Whatever you want to say, I don't want to hear it, William Bettencourt. You were my friend, and you betrayed me, just like Mia did. I trusted you, and you plotted with her to betray me! Why would you do that, William?" I could hardly believe all the anger that I heard in my own voice. I really felt these emotions—in a hard, bitter and surprising way. Maybe William had meant more to me than I had thought.

"Don't hang up! Please, can we meet? I need to talk to you. You don't know everything. Mia is a dangerous woman, and I didn't betray you—I didn't dare leave her alone. By the time I knew she was serious, by the time I knew she was coming after you with a loaded gun, I couldn't leave her. That would have sent her over the edge!"

"You should have called me or called the police. How dare you call me now! I cared about you. Did you ever really care about me?" Tears slid down my cheeks. William had been my friend for three years. We'd flirted, tried to date and kissed once or twice, but it never worked out. He didn't answer me right away. Finally he asked, "Are you still a horrible singer?"

"What?"

"I said are you still a horrible singer?"

"Hell, yes I am. But what does that have to do with anything?"

"It's still me, CJ. It's William. I know you. And I have to say this—I've been dying to say this. I love you. I made a mistake by not telling you that. I made a mistake not telling you that I suspected Mia had a problem, but I am telling you now. Are you listening?"

"Yes, I'm listening."

"Mia thinks she's related to the Cottonwoods. Something about some guy named Jeremiah; she's related to him some kind of way. Anyway, she's been taking some kind of medication or a drug—I don't even know if it's legal. It's supposed to help her...what's it called again...'dream catch,' kind of like you. She's been sleeping with all kinds of things around her bed, but mostly she would just wake up screaming and cursing. She could do what you do, and it drove her crazy. She said she saw pictures and blurs of color but nothing clear and nothing that made sense. All she could do was feel things, feel the anger of Jeremiah."

"Are you joking? Is this part of some new scam, William?"

"Shut up and listen." He sounded as serious as I had ever heard him. "I'm not scamming you, CJ. She's going to try and come at you again. She hasn't given up. This is a ruse for her to get close to you. Don't go see her, no matter how much her parents beg you."

"Next you'll be telling me that Alice and Myron are in on it." He didn't answer me, but I wouldn't let it go. "Is that what you're saying?"

"I don't know for sure, but I think they could be. Just let the law handle Mia. This place they have her in—it's what it is known as a low-security facility. That means without much effort, Mia could be out of it in no time. If she can get to you, she will."

"But why? To what end? The treasure has been found, William. And Seven Sisters belongs to Ashland, not me. Why would she come after me?"

In a steely, serious voice, he said, "I think she wants to kill you, Carrie Jo. She has this idea in her sick head that if she kills you and does some kind of ritual, something she learned in Egypt, she can have your powers after you die. I know it sounds crazy. I didn't want to believe it either, but there it is. I am telling you the truth. Please listen to me. Keep your friends close to you. Keep the doors locked. Don't let your guard down for a minute."

I sat on the floor, closing my front door with shaking hands. I could hardly believe what William had told me. What did it all mean?

"Carrie Jo, please. Can I come over? I'll keep watch with you. I want to keep you safe."

"No, William. I don't want to see you. Thanks for calling me and telling me what you know. I thank you for that, but there is no way I am going to trust you again. At least, not right now."

"I want you to trust me, CJ. I do love you, as I always have. You know I have. What I said to you that night on Dauphin Street, it was a lie. A big lie! I did come down here to be close to you. I came down here because I wanted to have more than a kiss with you. I love everything about you. Your smile, your horrible singing, your beautiful face. It's you I want. Why else would I still be talking to Mia? I had to watch over you the best way I knew how. Please say you'll give me a second chance."

"I'm seeing Ashland, William. I'm not the kind of girl to date two guys at once. I do thank you for calling me."

He sighed, sounding defeated. "Well, I wanted you to know. My best to your boyfriend, and please tell him what I told you. Stay safe, Carrie Jo."

"Thanks, William." I hung up the phone. I lay on the area rug and stared up at the pristine white, glossy ceiling. What just happened? How did that monkey wrench get tossed into my plans again?

I thought for a few minutes, then I got to my feet. When William and I were dating, I ended it because I realized I wasn't in love with him. No matter what he said, he couldn't talk me into being in love. It just wasn't there. Still, I felt grateful for the phone call. I tapped on the phone screen again, ready to call Ashland to fill him in.

"No, I better not," I said to no one in particular. If I called him, I wouldn't have the opportunity to do what I planned to do later.

Tonight would be the night. It was now or never. I would finally sleep at Seven Sisters. I hoped I knew what I was doing, or this might be the last nap I ever took.

I kept my eyes peeled for petite lurkers wielding knives or guns in the hedges as I went back and forth to the laundry room for the next few hours. The more I thought about it, the more ridiculous it all seemed. But I did my research. Mobile Mental Health was indeed a low-security facility, so that much was true. As for William being in love with me, that wasn't something I could help.

About 11 a.m., Detra Ann's email pinged my inbox. I clicked on the attachment and studied the letter that appeared on my screen. I was surprised to recognize the handwriting. David Garrett's. I'd "read" many of his letters to Calpurnia while I dreamed about her, so I'd seen that script before.

Dearest One,

It pains me to hear such disturbing reports about your behavior while I'm away. My sincere hopes had been that you would stop fighting me at every turn and allow the physicians to provide you with the ministrations you need to overcome this serious malady. Perhaps reading this note will put you in remembrance of the promise I made to you. "Never will I leave you, nor forsake you, not for a thousand treasures or for Aphrodite herself." You are my own Dear Love; have I not proven such?

Stop believing the things your eyes see, because we know they cannot be trusted. Do not listen to the things your ears hear, because I shall always love you, no matter what others may say. I desire only your happiness and peace.

I will return to you as soon as I land in Mobile. I have something to show you, something that may pique your interest. Wear the blue gown for me, Dearest One. How I love to see you in your finery once again! No more black.

With much admiration and love,

David

The back of the letter listed her address as Dauphin Street Hospital, her name, Iona Garrett. That was it. I sat back in amazement. No matter what I thought of the captain, I had to at least give him credit for coming up with the sister cover story and trying to get Isla some help. Not that it ever worked. I printed a copy of the letter and forwarded it to Ashland, who immediately wrote me back, "Wow! That's amazing. Must be Isla, right?"

I sent back a smiley face and agreed with him. I folded my clothing and kept my doors locked. Despite what William told me, I still intended to do what I had planned.

I would sleep at the house and no one, alive or dead, would stop me.

Chapter 15

Sitting in the driveway of Seven Sisters, I talked to Ashland. I prayed that an ambulance wouldn't go whizzing by and bust me. As far as he knew, I was safe at home in my apartment. I still hadn't told him about William, and the guilt was beginning to weigh on me. "Yes, I am turning in early."

"Hoping for some good dreams?"

"You know me. That's what I do, right?"

"No, that's not what you do. You are a researcher—a historian. This dreaming business, this is just extra. One day, when these mysteries are solved, you'll be able to turn them off, right?"

I sighed. "I hope so. I have never dreamed so much in my life, and I have never been so emotionally invested with a group of people who haven't been alive in well over a hundred years. I'm hoping this goes away. After this, I look forward to sleeping in a brand new house far away from downtown Mobile."

"I see. I'd like to get to know that girl, the one that doesn't dream and sleeps in a new home away from Seven Sisters. And I've been thinking..."

"Long trip? Nothing better to do?"

"Hey, cut that out. I think all the time, not just on long, boring trips."

I chuckled, grateful that he had a sense of humor about the whole thing. "So what have you been thinking?"

"I've been thinking that we need to set a deadline. If we don't know something by Halloween, we let it go. We can't let this absorb our lives. I don't want it to do to you what it did to my mother. Me either. We have to live a real life with birthday parties and spaghetti dinners. We have to be real people, Carrie Jo. I need to be real."

"I am so glad you said that." Happy tears filled my eyes. This was exactly what I had been feeling when we spoke last, but I couldn't articulate it like he had. "I love you, Ashland Stuart. Not your old name or your money. Not your football trophies or your amateur detective skills. I love you."

"And I needed to hear that. Thank you, Carrie Jo, for not laughing at me and for taking on my family mystery like it was your own. I don't know any other woman that would have done as much as you have. I love you too."

I smiled into the phone. I took a deep breath and stared up at the house in front of me. Seven Sisters practically glowed in the moonlight. Purple shadows flitted across the colonnade; they looked like fleeting dark spirits, but it was only the wind moving the branches off nearby trees. "I better go now, Ashland. I'm getting ready for bed. See you in the morning?"

"You know it. I know I said this once, but I love you, Carrie Jo Jardine."

"I love you too. Goodnight." I hung up, trying not to feel guilty about lying to the man I just declared my love for. This wasn't what I wanted. I grabbed my purse and my bag and locked my car. I parked it out of the way and out of the obvious view from the driveway, but I didn't park around back. That would be admitting guilt for sure.

I walked toward the house. It looked so different at night and felt different too, now that I was alone. The pots were the same, each filled with various flowers like hydrangeas and hibiscus. I stood on the porch, pushing my key in the door, and

I immediately went into wariness mode. I had no intention of being surprised by Mia with a weapon.

I wasted no time getting inside; at least I didn't have to look at the ugly satyr this time. I tapped in the alarm code, disarming the building, and then re-entered the code to arm it again. I checked the lights; all were lit and shining red. That meant locked down, right? I hoped so. Chip or Ashland normally handled the alarm system, but I thought I had done everything right. I didn't dare use a flashlight. Instead, I used my cell phone as a light as I walked across the foyer toward the spiral staircase. Calpurnia's room was upstairs, the first door on the right.

I climbed the creaking stairs, hoping I could avoid the usual squeaky spots with a little light footwork, but to no avail. *That meant that any mice who might be lurking about would know I was coming*, I thought in an attempt to amuse myself. *There was nothing hiding in the darkness here, right?* Bienville would be mightily ashamed.

Without pausing to think or worry, or look for unusual shadows, I pushed open the door. I had just been here the night before in my dreams, watching Calpurnia bathe in her gown. What a ridiculous custom that was! How happy was I to have a shower and the cultural permission to shower nude!

Still using my cell phone, I walked around the room and closed the blinds. I had pine- and cedar-scented candles in my bag, wanting to shed some needed light in the room. I had even brought a thrift store plate to put under them to catch the melting wax. I wanted to sleep, not wake up screaming in a dark room, but I didn't want to attract any attention. The heavy velvet curtains were drawn now, so it would be impossible for anyone to see candlelight. I hoped.

The bedroom was still arranged the way it had been after the supernatural activity there. I tried not to think about the sounds of scraping furniture and the sighing. I so wanted to believe it was Calpurnia who had moved her furniture around. When I closed the door, the sight of the lock made me sick to my stomach. It wasn't the original lock to this door, but it reminded me of all the times Mr. Cottonwood had locked his daughter in the room as punishment for one thing or another.

I set the candles on the nightstand. I lit the candles, and it immediately made the room look and smell happier. I stared at the door and knew I had to put something against it. I grabbed the desk chair and leaned it against the doorknob to prevent human intruders. What would I do if a spirit intruder arrived? I wouldn't think about that.

I left my clothes on, removing only my shoes and socks and tucking them in my bag. I pulled back the covers on Calpurnia's bed and lay down. It felt wrong being there, like I was an intruder in the girl's room, but maybe that was just me being me. I opened the last journal and began to read the next page.

Dear Diary,

Last night, as I waited to hear word from CG, I re-read the poetry book Uncle Louis last bought me. This poem, "The Will and the Wing" by Paul Hamilton Hayne speaks such stirrings to my soul! Listen to this, Dearest Diary...

To have the will to soar, but not the wings,
Eyes fixed forever on a starry height,
Whence stately shapes of grand imaginings
Flash down the splendors of imperial light;

And yet to lack the charm that makes them ours,
The obedient vassals of that conquering spell,
Whose omnipresent and ethereal powers
Encircle Heaven, nor fear to enter Hell;
This is the doom of Tantalus – the thirst
For beauty's balmy fount to quench the fires
Of the wild passion that our souls have nurst
In hopeless promptings – unfulfilled desires.
Yet would I rather in the outward state
Of Song's immortal temple lay me down,
A beggar basking by that radiant gate,
Than bend beneath the haughtiest empire's crown!
For sometimes, through the bars, my ravished eyes
Have caught brief glimpses of a life divine,
And seen afar, mysterious rapture rise
Beyond the veil that guards the inmost shrine.

Oh yes, to have the will to soar but not the wings! What sheer agony that would have been! Not I! I have both the Will and the Wind! My Will is my own, but my Wind, that will toss the sails and push us together toward our destiny.

Tonight, my Own Dear, tonight I confess my heart to you, for I know you have long waited to hear me say these words. I shall surprise you! I shall surprise you indeed, and you will welcome me into your strong arms and promise me that all will be well, yes, all shall be well.

The house is quiet tonight. Isla has left for a night of fun and foolishness with Ocie. I bid her good riddance. May she be as happy here as I was! Muncie waits for my instructions. My dark blue cloak and hood are already stowed in the barn in my horse's stall. I have shoved several coins into my change purse. I liberated twenty such coins from my father's purse easily enough. He was stone drunk on corn whiskey. Now the coins are in my purse, tied to my wrist. This small fortune would take care of us for an entire year at least, surely. I have no head for figures. I have given up on finding Mother's Treasure, but at least I will have her name, for that will be the name I travel with. I am no longer Calpurnia Cottonwood but Christine Beaumont. Once I marry, I will be Christine Garrett, wife of Captain David Garrett.

I have everything planned out. I have been sending Muncie on false runs into town. Actually, he has been racing the horse down to the river to the Delta Queen. He's gotten the time perfect now, and we are almost ready to run. Tonight will be the night! The steamboat will leave the dock at 8, and we don't want to arrive too early. It would be best if we were puffing up the Mobile River before my father discovered I was missing. As much corn whiskey as I fed him tonight, he may never wake up again. Forgive me for hoping so!

Here I am now, tapping my foot nervously. I've paced the floor. I've taken great pains to hide my journals in the floorboards, in case things don't go as I have planned. My book of notes from my Captain I have tucked inside my purse. And you, my Dear Diary, I shall truly miss. I write to you hastily now because you too must be hidden from prying eyes.

Au Revoir, Dearest Diary! When next you hear from me, I shall certainly be Mrs. David Garrett, world explorer and woman of the world!

I closed the book and closed my eyes and soon drifted off to sleep. I imagined Calpurnia kissing the book and hiding it. She no doubt wore her coral-colored gown because as Garrett had written in one of his notes, that was his favorite dress of hers. Then I felt myself sinking, sinking into the world of the past...I whispered to myself, "Captain David Garrett," over and over again. I had to get this right.

I lay there for what seemed like hours, but sleep didn't come. I swore under my breath and eventually just got up. This had been a stupid idea, anyway, hadn't it? Might as well go home and get some real sleep.

Before I blew out the candles, I walked to the mirror. My face wasn't staring back at me—it was Calpurnia's. She didn't seem to notice that I was there at all. I said something to her, and I saw her shiver and look about her. She ignored it, dabbed perfume on her wrists and neck and poked a few more pearl-tipped pins into her hair. I breathed slowly, reminding myself to watch only, not interfere. My job was to watch and learn.

It couldn't hurt, could it?

I slid my feet into the satin shoes with the low heels and walked out of the room. Hooney caught me outside. "You going somewhere, Miss?"

"Why yes, Hooney. I'm going to visit with Ocie. I won't be gone too long. Oh dear, is it that late? Well, then I won't be back until morning, I'm afraid."

"What about your Father? Mr. Cottonwood will be fit to be tied if he finds out that you..."

"Now, no worrying. You let me worry about him. It's only for a late supper and some quilting. I am sure Father wouldn't mind that. I am going to be an old married lady soon. I hope he understands that ladies like to spend time with other ladies before they marry."

"Oh yes," she said with a chuckle, "you should do that. You need that now that your Momma is gone, God rest that Angel's soul! You go on and have a time with those ladies. I'll send Stokes for the horse."

"No, Muncie will take care of it all. He knows which my favorite is, and I would like him to serve me." I didn't make eye contact but pretended to smooth my dress and hair as Hooney called for Muncie.

"Now, boy!" Muncie arrived just as we planned and I climbed up on the horse to ride sidesaddle supposedly to Ocie's.

"Here, let us get the carriage, ma'am. How will you ride home?" Hooney called up, looking worried and suspicious.

"Ocie's father will allow me to use his carriage, I'm sure. Now I must go. Time is wasting. Goodnight." I whispered into Muncie's ear, "Get me out of here."

We rode down the lane at an easy gallop but stopped once we left their sight. He handed me my cloak and hood. Where we were going, nobody needed to know that it was me—until I was ready to reveal myself. I wrapped the cloak around myself, and he lifted me back up into the saddle.

"Thank you, my friend. When you leave me, I want you to go right to Reginald Ball's camp. You remember the one, it's on the other side of the river. The one the Cottonwoods use all the time. Father rarely goes there anymore, but Mr. Ball says he paints there when he wants peace and quiet. Tell him what I have done, and give him the letter I wrote for you. As a married woman, I can grant you your freedom, and I know my husband will approve. You will be a free man, but get to Reginald. He is a good man. He will help us free you. I want to protect you from my father's whip. You will remember, Muncie?"

"Yes, I'll remember. Let's ride now so we don't miss the boat."

"Yes, let's ride." I clung to the horn of the saddle for all I was worth, the blue cloak swirling around me. We passed only one other rider, and he barely acknowledged us or looked in our direction.

At the dock, we pulled the horse into some woods and tied him to a tree. I removed my cloak and straightened my coral gown and patted my hair. Muncie's worried face gave me pause. I couldn't bear it if my friend were to suffer on my account. I wrapped my arms around his neck and gave him a quick hug. "Thank you for everything. I will write to Reginald, so please let him know where you shall be. I want to stay in touch, Muncie."

He just nodded and stared at the ground, surely at a loss for words. I knew he was the kind of boy—no, man—who had deep feelings for his friends. I knew he that was worried for me and that he loved me as the true friend he was. Still, I couldn't linger, I walked along the gangplank, pausing as I did. Here it was. The night I had been waiting for! The night where all things would become possible for me. With a sweet smile and a tiny wave of my fingers, I said "Goodbye" to him, maybe for the last time.

The picture began to fade into the distance, and I could hear someone screaming, screaming my name. "Carrie JO-O-O-O!" I shook myself awake, angry that the dream had broken at such a crucial moment. But then my anger was quickly replaced with fear. I was more than startled to see Mia sitting on the edge of the bed with a black leather strap in her hands.

"My, my, my. What a bit of a pickle you've gotten yourself into, CJ. Bit of a pickle, bit of a pickle, bit of a pickle." She was laughing wildly, and I sat up cautiously. "Doesn't that sound funny? So funny."

"Mia, what are you doing here? You shouldn't be here. How did you escape the hospital?"

"How do you think? I had help, of course. You are far too trusting, Carrie Jo. Far too trusting. You'll never believe who's been helping me. Are you ready for this? Give me a drum roll, please!" I just stared at her; I certainly wasn't going to give her a drum roll. I was thinking about how I could get out of this room without getting smacked with that belt.

"Well, I'll save that for later. For now, you might be wondering how I got in here, right?" I nodded obediently. "That secret door there, dummy. You never were much of a researcher, were you?" She laughed again at my perceived stupidity.

"Sugar is sweet and so are you. Sugar is sweet and so are you, CJ." She swung around the pole of the four-poster, obviously under the influence of some kind of drug. And armed. "Oh so sweet. I hear you and Ashland have been kissing in a tree, K-I-S-S-I-N-G! I knew it right from the beginning that you had your eye on him, but who can blame you? That guy is hot—and loaded, don't forget loaded!" She laughed and laughed as if she couldn't help herself.

"What do you want, Mia? Why are you here?"

"Oh, why am I here? Why are *you* here?" She cracked the belt by her side. She didn't hit me, but I could see where the tail of the belt had left a welt on her hand. A thin trail of blood appeared, but Mia didn't even seem to notice. "When I came up here to play around, you had me fired. That was rich, wasn't it? Now you know you heard Isla's voice in here, but you just couldn't stand that I might have more powers than you. You took Seven Sisters away from me—and Ashland too!"

"No, I never did!" I got out of the bed, wishing there was some way I could get to my phone without her seeing me. "I didn't ask for this, Mia. It's not something I prayed for or did some kind of spell to get. It just happens. You know that!"

"You *know* that!" she repeated, mocking me to my face. "Stop whining, girl. I hate hearing you whine constantly about dreaming. What great irony God has—if there is a God! Someone who doesn't want to see the past is a dream catcher, while someone who would give her soul for the ability can't have it. But I *can* have it and I will! I never wanted any damn hidden treasure. That was Isla! I never wanted Ashland either! You have the treasure. It's inside you, just waiting for someone like me to come scoop it out." Mia dropped the belt and slid a knife out of her pocket. She flipped it open, the silver blade shimmering dangerously in the candlelight.

"Mia, you don't know what you're saying. I'm your friend, remember. It was you and me and William. We're your friends. He called me, told me about how worried he was. I am too. Please let us help you."

She laughed again, an ugly, low sound. "William told you what I told him to tell you. That is all. As a matter of fact, why don't you meet our special guest tonight? Come on out, baby. She knows you're here." Mia snatched the chair away from the door, sending it to the ground with a crash. She turned the brass key and unlocked the door. I peered into the blackness and saw no one.

"Come on, baby. Don't be shy."

William stepped into the doorway, a devilish grin on his face. He didn't look at me, just Mia.

"Say hello to our guest, baby."

"Hello," William whispered. The small grin remained on his lips, and his dark eyes sparkled with amusement. He'd betrayed me again, and I had believed him. If I weren't in fear of being stabbed to death by Mia's blade, I would have fallen to the floor.

Chapter 16

Mia paced the room, waving her blade as she talked. "You know, I see things too. You aren't the only one with special blood and powers, Carrie Jo Jardine. But I am stronger, much stronger than you and soon I'll be even stronger than you.. Then I can go anywhere, and I can dream about the ancient times, in faraway places. I will do it, and you will be dead. How does that sound?" She had stopped her facing and was just inches from my face.

"It doesn't sound very good, Mia. Please, stop this." I tried to think of something to say that would keep her busy, but nothing came to mind. My eyes searched the room. How would I get out of here? William blocked the door, and Mia stood between me and the secret passage.

"I'm going to give you a choice, CJ. We can do this the easy way or the hard way; which way do you prefer?" Her finger touched the tip of the knife, and I could see the blood drip as she cut herself. "You can lie down like a good girl and go to sleep, or we can take out what we need while you kick and scream. Which would you like?" She took a step toward me.

"Mia, don't do this," I said, gasping with raw emotion. "Please!"

"Uh, uh, uh. That's not the right answer. Try again. Will you cooperate, or shall we have a bit of fun?" She swung her blade at me and laughed. William stood in the doorway, not moving, just watching the drama unfold.

"William, how could you do this?" I yelled at him. "Are you just going to stand there and let her murder me? You told me you loved me, remember that? Did you ever love me?" I saw something flicker in his eyes. Regret, maybe? Anger? How was this happening?

Mia growled with anger. "He never told you he loved you! He's never been yours, CJ. He's mine! You can't have everything. Not everything" Her breath was hot on my skin.

"No, Mia! Don't do this!" I put my hands up above my head, waiting for the knife blade to make contact when suddenly the air shifted and I could feel a strange vibration. In a split second the candles sailed through the air, pelting Mia with hot wax and flames but it wasn't William that tossed them at my attacker. Someone unseen was helping me. She screamed, and I climbed over her and then took off running with all my might toward the secret door. Out of the corner of my eye, I saw William race toward me, then a surprised look crossed his face as a ghostly hand crashed something that looked like a wooden stick down upon him. I screamed and ran pell-mell into the darkness.

"Oh God, oh God, oh God! Help me!" I ran, wondering who or what was following me. I had no idea where I was going, and I gasped in panic as I navigated the small space.

"CJ! Wait, I'm on your side!" It was William, and he wasn't too far behind me. "Please wait. I love you, CJ!"

Liar! Damn, liar! I wanted to scream but I didn't answer him. I kept running. I turned left, then right and then left again until I came to a dead end. My hands flew over the dusty wall, looking for a lever or a brace of some kind. I couldn't die here, not inside the walls of Seven Sisters where no one would ever find me. I didn't cry out or scream, and even though the blackness made moving slower than I wanted the darkness hid me. I gasped to keep the scream suppressed and pounded on the wall, hoping that I might trigger something. How was I going to get out of here?

Oh, Ashland! I should have told you what I planned to do. You'll never find me now. Never! I'm done for with these two.

All of a sudden, William stood beside me. I could see his outline in the darkness. "William, don't hurt me. Please, don't. You don't want to do that. I thought you were my friend!"

His voice was soft and reassuring as he raised his hands. I could barely see them in the shadowy space. "I would never harm you, Carrie Jo. I am here to protect you, remember?" His hand reached out, and I thought he was going to touch me, but he reached past me to something high on the wall. He pulled a hidden knob and opened the door to Louis Beaumont's room. Somehow we had ended up on the other side of the house. The room was bright from the moonlight streaming in through curtainless windows. I could see William smile down at me. Could it be true? Was he my friend?

From behind him I heard a growl. Mia thrust her blade into his back, and I could see the shock cross William's face. He fell to his knees, and Mia wore a triumphant smile behind him. "Traitor," she declared over him. "That's what happens to traitors~ Well, it looks like you weren't the only fool in this game, CJ." Blood was streaming down like some invisible hand had turned on a bloody water faucet.

"Oh no, William! Mia, what have you done? Stop it!"

William slid to the floor with a moan and after a few seconds didn't move at all. The dark red blood oozed out of his back and onto the floor. Mia stepped over him and lunged towards me. I was next on her list and she wasn't going to be happy until I was dead. Completely and utterly annihilated.

"Now where were we, CJ? I remember! You were about to die, and I was about to get your powers." Mia grinned at me and tossed the knife from hand to hand. I could see painted symbols on her bare arms, strange painted symbols, a few looked like hieroglyphics. Did she really believe that by killing me she would gain my dreamcatching powers?

"We need to help William, Mia. Stop this! What about Alice and Myron? They are concerned for you—they love you! It's not too late, Mia!"

"Oh but it is. William is beyond help now. He's a betrayer. He betrayed us both. I guess that makes him a double betrayer. Those are the worst kind, Carrie Jo. Now lie down here and let's get this over with. Why make it hard on yourself? I'm going to get what I came for and then maybe I'll pay Ashland a visit. He's got a few skills I'd like to harness," she laughed but it wasn't a pleasant sound. Not at all.

I moved away from her slowly walking backward so I could keep my eye on her and that knife. William still wasn't moving and I couldn't tell if he was breathing or not. "No, Mia!" I picked up a cordless phone and threw it at her. I grabbed whatever I could off the desk and sent it sailing her in her direction. Where was my ghost friend now? She laughed and dodged everything easily, never ceasing her pursuit of me.

I reached for the doorknob, only to discover the door was locked. Who had locked the door? I tugged on the knob and fumbled with the latch. Mia was right behind me; I turned to look into her crazy dark eyes, to face my death with my back against the door. *What next? What do I do next? This is how I will die, right here at Seven Sisters. I'll become a ghost like Christine and Calpurnia. Who could come collect me? Isla? David Garrett?*

Mia raised the knife above her head as I closed my eyes and screamed and suddenly, a shot rang out. Instinctively, I ducked to the ground and watched as Isla's arm dropped, and she stood swaying on her feet. She looked confused, and then a strange blankness crossed her face. Before she crumpled to the ground, she asked, "CJ?" I looked beyond her and saw William lying on the floor with a gun in his hand. From somewhere he'd pulled that weapon and I had never known he had it. He had shot Mia and saved my life. I ran to him, picking up the phone I had thrown along the way.

"William, stay with me. Okay? Stay with me!" I pulled off my shirt and pressed it against the wound on his back, trying to stop the bleeding. With shaking fingers I dialed 9-1-1 and gave our information. "William, I have to go unlock the front door. You stay awake and hold this phone. Hold this phone, and don't you dare go to sleep! You got it?"

"Yes," he whispered.

I side-eyed Mia but she didn't move. I raced down the stairs and to the door, disarming the alarm and unlocking the bolt. I left the door wide open and ran back up. Nothing to fear now; the evil that had chased me was now dead in a heap on the floor. Mia's eyes stared into nothingness but then I saw her blink. No, she was not dead, she was hanging on if for no other reason than to try to kill me again. Death was close by, I could feel it. I panicked as I saw William's eyes begin to flutter.

"William! William Bettencourt! Don't you dare go to sleep! I'm here. I'm with you!" I wanted to cry, to scream for help, but I knew help was on the way. I feared it would be too late.

"Carrie Jo, I'm sorry. I tried to help. Everything I do is wrong."

I held the bloody rag to his back and smiled at him as if nothing were wrong, "Stop talking, William. You need to be quiet. Listen, the sirens are getting closer. Can you hear them?"

"I love you, Carrie Jo. I have always loved you."

"I know, William. I love you too," I lied to him. "It's all going to be all right. You'll see."

William smiled, and his eyes blinked and lowered—the smile still on his face.

"No, no. William, please don't die. Please! William!" I began to cry; I held his head in my lap and smoothed his dark curls with my bloody fingers. I watched as his life slipped away from him.

What do I do now?

Suddenly, in a rush of activity, an emergency team was in the room, pulling me away from him. They worked on William for a minute, and then hastily transported him to the ambulance. Someone handed me a jacket, and I remembered I was wearing only a bra. My bloody shirt lay wadded on the floor. Another team worked at stabilizing Mia who was moaning and crying.

I sat on the floor, unsure of what to do. Go with William? No, he was dead now. I certainly wasn't going to go with Mia. I could hear the sirens wailing down the driveway taking him to the hospital. I looked up to find Detective Simmons staring at me.

"So we meet again. What is it about this house, Miss Jardine? Dead bodies just keep showing up here. Or maybe it's not the house at all but something else." She squatted down beside me. I knew what she meant, but she was wrong. It wasn't entirely me. It wasn't the house, either. It was the past—it was a bevy of spirits struggling toward their desired destinies even beyond their life's allowance of years. Strange to think that the human will could be so strong but it could be. Isla Beaumont was proof and so was Mia Reed. But I couldn't tell her that. I didn't bother.

I stood up. "I'm going to the hospital to see William. We'll talk later, or you can follow me there."

I walked out of Seven Sisters maybe for the last time.

At this moment, I never wanted to return to the house—it had taken too much from me. Too much had been lost. Yet, I knew that I would one day. That I must because nothing was settled. Not really. How they had all struggled against their fate, Christine, Louis, Calpurnia—even Ann-Sheila. In my own time, Hollis, Mia, William, and TD. I had done all I could do to prevent those old spirits from forcing their way into our lives, but they had done just that.

From now on, I would no longer welcome the past into my world. I would do my best to shut it out, to refuse it access. I could no longer give my life away just to peer into theirs. Ashland had been right. This had been a bad idea, and now William had paid for my foolishness.

I was done with dreaming. Or so I thought.

Epilogue

Before my mind knew what I was doing, my heart had plunged me into the cold river. We'd had a cool snap recently, and the chill had settled in the water. I dove into the dark water, praying all the way. I saw her frail body crash into the black, her bright dress sink below the water, the weight of it pulling her down, down, down to her death. I rose once to breathe and could hear people on the boat shouting, but I didn't care. I dove down deeper, struggling against the current. It ran strong and fierce tonight, although you'd never see that from the surface.

I came up for air once more, and then dove again, this time following the current. Thank goodness the stars shone bright and the moon glowed that night or I would have never seen her. She hung in the water like a magical hovering creature, still and unmoving. Her body traveled past the boat almost to the other shore. I swam to her, ignoring everything else—all my fears of snakes and gators. I surfaced once more for air, glanced at the boat and saw Mr. Ball pointing at the water.

I dove again and grabbed Calpurnia by her narrow waist and hoisted her to the surface. The gown indeed weighed her down but there was nothing for it. I struggled with all my might to get her to safety. Behind me there were a half-dozen splashes in the water, but I didn't look back at a single one of them. I swam to the shore and shoved her onto the muddy banks. There were no lights here, nothing to help me see her, but I laid her on her back. She wasn't breathing, and her face was white as a sun-beaten sheet.

I shook her and said her name over and over. "Please, Calpurnia. Don't be dead. You can't be dead. Wake up, wake up now." I whispered as I shook her. I glanced over my shoulder toward the boat but from what I could see they didn't see us at all but there were more splashes in the water. They would find us eventually. Calpurnia didn't speak or move or flutter an eyelash. I remembered seeing a drowning before. Early had nearly died once but Stokes had slapped him back to life. I turned her on her side and patted her back, not too hard but firmly, to ease the water out of her. At first nothing happened, but then I heard a strangling sound and Callie began to retch river water out of her body.

"Oh, thank you, Lord. Thank you, Lord."

I continued to pat her until she had spewed up all the water. I heard a horse approach, and my mind said, "Run!" but my aching body could not comply. The horse came to a stop, and I looked up at the rider walking towards us. It was Reginald Ball, the gentleman who had painted Calpurnia last spring. He squatted down beside her and lifted her up.

"Are you alive, Miss Cottonwood?"

She nodded, coughing some more but never speaking.

"That was a very foolish thing to do. Very foolish indeed, but there is nothing to be done now. We must...um...I know where we can go. Muncie, can you walk? I don't think the three of us will fit on my horse."

"Yes, sir. I can run if I have to," I declared bravely as I continued to pant for breath. I had saved my friend but felt sick myself. How much of that river had I swallowed? My mouth tasted dirty, like river water and my eyes were burning.

"You will have to because I can hear the dogs now. Let's go to my camp and get her tended to. Help me hoist her onto my horse. Can you help us, Calpurnia? That's a good girl. You can do it."

We lifted her together; she was awake but still hovering near unconsciousness. And she still didn't speak to us. Finally, Calpurnia was atop the horse, with Mr. Ball holding her close. I did as I was told and ran after them barefoot through the thick woods. I stepped on one thing and then another but I couldn't stop to doctor them up. I could hear the dogs barking now. Oh, those mean devils were close. A few times, Mr. Ball paused to allow me to catch up but he needn't have bothered. There was no way I was letting those hounds tear me apart. We traveled about two miles deep into the woods until we came upon a small cabin. I was never so glad to see a place as I was that one.

"This your place, Mister?" I said nervously as I licked my ferociously dry lips. I was certain anyone close would be able to hear the pounding of my heart. That would certainly give us away. Certainly it would.

"Yes, no one will bother us out here, young man. You have nothing to worry about, at least for a while. Help me lift her, oh dear. She's passed out. That's it. Thank you, Marcus" I took Calpurnia in my arms and carried her into the camp house. I didn't bother correcting Mr. Ball. Did it matter what he called me? Muncie? Marcus? Neither of these were my true name. My tired feet slapped heavily on the wooden boards and I quickly made my way to the small bed in the corner. As gently as I could I laid her on the bed, and Mr. Ball fussed about lighting a lamp, finding blankets, patting her awake. Finally, after much cajoling her eyes opened and he tried again to talk to her, but she wouldn't respond. It was like she couldn't see us or something. My heart was heavy as I plunked down into the chair by the window. I couldn't figure out which way to look, at Calpurnia or at the road outside. At least I didn't hear those dogs anymore. I wasn't sure she

could see us; her eyes might see something we couldn't, something faraway and sad.

"Please, Miss Calpurnia. Tell me what happened." She said nothing. Once in a while her eyes would look at mine, but she didn't see me. Or anything, not the dirty lamp, not her rustic surroundings. No. She didn't speak but sunk deeper into herself, kind of like her mother did. I prayed that what happened to Mrs. Cottonwood would not happen to her daughter but that was all I could do. No, she did not see me. Not that day or the next. Mr. Ball left us alone that night and one more but returned the day after with food, water and some money. It was good that he trusted me, but it also worrying. Each time he left I felt sick. Each time he returned I felt even sicker. I could not see who it was that approached until they were almost in the house. Mr. Ball looked worried and tired. I quietly repented for everything I had previously thought about him. He had proven to be a true friend and a good man. It was nice to know that Calpurnia had at least two people who cared about her.

"Everyone is looking for Miss Cottonwood, Marcus, but I haven't the heart to send her back to her father. If anyone knew—if they discovered that I had aided her or helped a runaway slave escape, I would be in jail. Probably hanged. Yet, I cannot sentence her to die. Nor you, good man," he patted my hand and smiled sadly. "He would kill Calpurnia if she returned after shaming him in such a way. Poor girl. I think I can make him see reason eventually, but it will take some time. We need to find a place for you both, far away from here but I don't risk taking her to Mobile proper. No, we can't take that risk."

"What do you mean shame him? She would never do such a thing."

He nodded at me to follow him to the other room. "Apparently she threw herself at the captain. She wanted to marry him, but he was already entertaining another lady. So heartbroken was she that she ran slap off the boat and into the water. Miss Calpurnia fell for the wrong sort of man. I always knew that man was a dishonest sort of fellow. And after all that she's been through already...well, there's nothing to be done for it now. How I wish she had married me when her mother was still alive. I am afraid that will not happen now."

"But he was to marry her. That captain promised her marriage. That was the plan. Can't she marry you now? She's a good girl, and you could protect her."

Mr. Ball paused before answering me, "Look at her, Marcus. She's in no condition to marry anyone."

"People call me Muncie, sir."

His eyebrows raised and he apologized. "I am sure I knew that but I as I said before, her father is in no mood to entertain new suitors, or anyone at all for that matter. He's as furious as I have ever seen him. And the captain, Mr. Cottonwood beat him within an inch of his life. It was a sight to see, and how the cousin wailed. I wonder if I should talk to the sheriff and ask him to intervene on Miss Calpurnia's behalf. If this has all been a mistake, a ruse played on her, obviously Garrett hoped to lay his hands upon her fortunes then surely her name would be cleared. Oh, how foolish! I tried to warn her, but she wouldn't listen. Still, Mr. Cottonwood cannot be allowed to harm her."

Warm bile rose in my throat at the thought of Callie being left in the sheriff's hands. "No! You can't call on the sheriff. He's not a friend. He punished Ann-Sheila, did things to her that no man should do to a woman. No, please, we cannot call the sheriff." Then

I did something I never did. I reached out and took his hands, squeezing them. "Please." He didn't push me away.

"You've been a kind friend to our Calpurnia." He patted my hand and nodded. "Very well. I will not, but we must think of another way forward. Where could I send her? She would be recognized in any home in this county, she is a renowned beauty and they've even put her description in the newspaper." He tapped his lip with his fat finger. "We'll have to travel by night, wherever we go."

We talked into the night, Calpurnia never moving, not even to relieve herself or take some food. We let her sleep, but I promised myself that I would have her eat that next morning no matter what.

Mr. Ball decided that Calpurnia and I would travel by ship somewhere, the destination to be chosen another time. He would do his best to reason with Mr. Cottonwood. Mr. Langdon didn't want to marry her now that she'd run off with a slave but he would. Mr. Ball hadn't given up hope in marrying her but Callie had to get well before we could take her anywhere. She would have to walk and speak and take care of herself. A black man, no slave, could go around carrying a white woman in public. Yes, she would have to walk and talk and be sensible. "In the meantime, keep her warm and comfortable. Get her to eat." Mr. Ball rose from the wooden table and smiled at me. "It's going to be all right, dear boy. We shall get through this. I still think I should notify the authorities, just to be on the safe side."

"No! You can't! The sheriff is a friend of Mr. Cottonwood, and he won't care if he kills her. Don't do it, Mr. Ball, please." He looked less sure of his earlier promise, but there was nothing else I could do to convince him. I could see his commitment wavering.

"*Very well, I shall return tomorrow after dark or perhaps the following day. There is plenty of food here and fresh clear water in the spring behind the house.*"

"*Thank you. Thank you, Mister.*"

He gave Calpurnia a sad look, put his hat on and walked out. I heard the horse ride away and turned to my friend. I had to break through to her. We couldn't wait for Mr. Ball to return. We had to leave as soon as we could! I would take her home, to my home. I would be Janjak again. Momma would help us. I know she would. My heart raced in my chest at this daring idea.

"*Callie, Miss...please, wake up.*" She stirred a little but never woke. Calm, keep calm, I told myself. Let her rest, and then you will talk. Explain to her everything that has happened, and then run, run for your lives! All through the night, I lay on the floor next to the fireplace, but I didn't dare to start a fire. And I didn't dare to sleep. I couldn't even if I wanted to. But it was so cold tonight. Maybe a small fire?

"*No, stupid. Don't be stupid,*" I could almost hear Hooney's berating tone in my ear.

What if someone saw the smoke? About the time morning cracked the sky, I heard her voice, "*Muncie? Where are we?*"

"*We're safe, Callie. I'm here, right here. We are in Mr. Ball's cabin. He has helped us to get away from the river.*" I came and sat beside her as she sat up, her hands shaking, her shoulders trembling. Her once fine gown was a crumpled mess of fabric.

"*Oh, I remember now. Oh, no I remember. I think I am going to be sick.*" I helped her out of the bed and to the front door. She threw up water and bile, off the side of the porch. I would have to wash that away if we were to stay.

"I'm okay, I am fine. I can walk, Muncie." She walked back inside like a brand new baby calf. I tore a piece of bread from the loaf and handed it to her. Callie wrinkled her nose at the offering.

"This will help you. Eat it, miss."

"I don't want to eat anything."

"You don't have any choice. We have to leave here and soon because I think Mr. Ball will bring the sheriff here this afternoon or tonight. If you don't eat, you won't have the strength to go. And we have to go."

Calpurnia took a bite of the bread and put the rest of the slice on the wooden table beside her. Her hands flew to her greasy hair and she did her best to improve her appearance. It wasn't working. She was paler than pale and looked sicker than sick. "What? He's going to bring the sheriff? Why? I have done nothing wrong."

"I suspect that the lawman would say otherwise. You know how he is, Callie. He is an evil man. And you are a runaway, and so am I. The whole city of Mobile is looking for us, right now. The whole county even. Mr. Ball is trying to reason with Mr. Cottonwood, but he's not having any luck. I think Mr. Ball is ready to give up; he's afraid that they will hang him from a limb. He's powerfully afraid of that."

"How long have we been here?" she asked as she swallowed some water from the cup I handed her.

"Three days now. This is the third day, I think."

"What's Mr. Ball trying to do? Where has he gone?" Calpurnia munched on the bread and stared at me.

"He wants to marry you so he can protect you and I can be free."

She stopped in mid-bite and swallowed. "No! I will never marry him nor anyone! No! I have to go!" She tried to leave but began to cry. "I shall never marry. I will die in that house. I know I will. Seven Sisters will be my prison, just like Mother..."

"No, no, you won't. Listen, you get strong. Eat your food. Tonight, after the sun goes down, and before he gets here we will go to the shipyard ourselves. Maybe I can trade some labor for passage. We can go to Haiti, to my home. I have people that will protect us there. My Momma and her sisters will protect us from harm."

"Do you think we can make it there?"

"I think so. Yes, we have to make it. Even if we have to walk the whole way."

She clutched my hand and leaned her head on my shoulder. "Yes, Muncie. I will eat and we will go, but you don't have to do labor. I have money, here." She felt her skirts, locating a hidden pocket and pulling out a purse. With shaking fingers, she opened the purse and dumped the contents onto the small bed. Coins bounced around, and a small book plopped on the ground. It was still damp from the river. I suspected that those pages were ruined now. I reached down and handed it to her. She accepted it and stared at it.

"You don't know what this is, do you?"

"No, I don't. What is it?"

"It's a book of lies. Lies a man told to a stupid girl. I swear to you, Muncie. If there were a fire in that fireplace, I would throw it in there and burn it from my memory. I am not going to die this way." She flopped on the bed and stared at the empty fireplace. "He never loved me, and I loved a dream. When I opened the door, he was with her. He was naked with her. It had all been a game to them."

I knew who she meant without her saying so. I sighed sadly. "Some men don't deserve happiness, and with her he will never find it. Isla is no man's woman but every man's. She will be the death of him, as she intended this to be for you."

She shoved the book into her bag and counted the coins, refusing to say more about it. We huddled in the cabin, hearing the dogs twice. But they never came close, not yet. It would only be a matter of time, though, before they discovered our hiding place. We were like the rabbits, waiting to be eaten. After the sun went down, we traveled through the woods. I knew the way. I knew how to read the moon and the stars and seek them for direction. This I learned from books. To our mutual surprise the docks were not far, not at all. I almost jumped for joy at seeing them but then I remembered the first trip here. The first time I'd ever been on a ship. Oh, but this would not be like that. I was going home. For sure, I was going home to Mama.

After midnight, we could see the port and the lights shimmering from the ships. I squeezed her hand. "Are you ready?"

"Yes, I am ready. Come what may, I am ready." We stepped onto the shell-covered road and walked toward the Harbormaster's office. Now was the moment of truth. We would live or we would die, but at least we would be together.

***

I woke to the low hum of the airplane's engine. I sat up and lifted the window shade. As we flew over the vast blue ocean, I wondered when we would make our descent into Haiti. Ashland was rereading the school's brochure, as he'd done a hundred times already. This was Janjak's school, or at least it had been founded by him. Now we were going to see it for ourselves, and Ashland had plans to make a sizable gift to the organization. We would walk where Janjak had walked and would at long last see the final resting place of Calpurnia Cottonwood. She'd died on the island, but much later. She'd lived a good life teaching and exploring the islands. Who knows what kind of happiness she found, but at least they were free—both of them.

"Not dreaming, are you?"

"I'll never tell," I purred, cuddling up to his arm.

"Then go back to sleep. We have a few more minutes before we land. You didn't sleep much last night." He kissed my forehead and leaned back in the seat. Once again I cuddled up next to him and dreamed, but not about the past this time.

No, this was different. It was bright and warm, this was a dream about the future—my future.

I looked down at my hands and noticed my perfect manicure and an heirloom wedding ring on my finger. I walked through a bright and airy room, hearing the soft cry of a baby, waking up surprised to find himself alone. "Now, now, I hear you, little man."

I pulled back the bassinet cover and smiled down at the round-faced baby with big blue eyes. For a moment, I felt them beside me, but I felt no fear. I didn't need to look. I knew who they were.

I hoped Calpurnia knew that the curse had been broken and that we were all free now. Free from all the dark shadows of Seven Sisters. We'd given the house to the City of Mobile. It was no longer ours. Our family was free forever.

I hoped Janjak knew that love, true love, always triumphs and that because of his selfless love, we were all here today, happy and safe and alive.

"Thank you," I whispered in my dream as I reached down and gathered my son—our son—in my arms.

Don't miss out!

Visit the website below and you can sign up to receive emails whenever M.L. Bullock publishes a new book. There's no charge and no obligation.

https://books2read.com/r/B-A-CXMC-FZPRB

BOOKS 2 READ

Connecting independent readers to independent writers.

Also by M.L. Bullock

Desert Queen Saga
The Tale of Nefret
The Falcon Rises
The Kingdom of Nefertiti
The Song of the Bee Eater

Devecheaux Antiques and Haunted Things Trilogy Series
Devecheaux Antiques and Haunted Things
A Cup of Shadows
A Voice From Her Past
A Watch Of Weeping Angels

Gulf Coast Paranormal Season Two
The Beast of Limerick House

Gulf Coast Paranormal Trilogy Series

Ghosted
Haunted
Dead
Spooked
Paranormal

Haunting Passions
For the Love of Shadows
Her Haunted Heart

Marietta
The Bones of Marietta
Footsteps of Angels

Scary Fall Stories
Horrible Little Things

Seven Sisters
Seven Sisters
Moonlight Falls On Seven Sisters
Ghost on a Swing

Watch for more at www.mlbullock.com.

About the Author

Author M.L. Bullock enjoys the laid-back atmosphere and the spooky vibe of the Gulf Coast, especially the region's historic districts and sites. When she isn't visiting her favorite haunts in New Orleans or Old Mobile, you can find her flipping through old photographs or newspaper clippings in search of new inspiration.

Read more at www.mlbullock.com.

Lightning Source UK Ltd.
Milton Keynes UK
UKHW021603040422
401067UK00008B/1474

9 798201 245474